MOON VINE

NIGHTGARDEN SAGA #2

LUCY HOLDEN

FEHU PRESS

For my sister, Lisa, with all my love

PROLOGUE

*H*ey, Tessa.

I can feel winter coming.

The moon vine I planted winds about my window, buds stubbornly closed during the day, unfurling like a silent secret when night falls. The flowers remind me of you, pale and delicate on the outside, but vibrant at their core. Like you, they're stronger than they look. Resilient. Willing to grow here even though they don't belong. That's how I often think of you. You smiled and laughed, even though part of you must always have known you couldn't stay long. I see your face every night as the petals unfold to reveal fathomless cores of indigo. I hear you whisper my name on the breeze that carries their scent through my window.

Sometimes I don't know what is real, anymore.

I always thought you'd be at my wedding. You weren't, though. Nobody was. It was just Antoine, me, and the priest he compelled to marry us. All I have to remind me it was real is a marriage certificate I keep hidden in a box under my bed, a bloodstained dress I can't bear to wash, and an emerald ring

1

Connor thinks is a family heirloom. It is. Just not one from my family.

It's the famous Marigny emerald, not that anyone knows. Who'd believe me, anyway?

The dreams have stopped. Since the title of the house was changed to my married name, Harper Marigny, I don't hear Keziah whisper to me anymore. Antoine said the magic in the binding spell protects the owner of the house from her mind control. I think she's still awake, though. I can feel her, a strange current on the air, as if she's waiting for something. I guess creatures like Keziah never stop waiting.

Creatures like Antoine.

Vampires.

I know what he is. But I can't think of him in the same way as Keziah. He was created to save people from what she and Caleb are, to defeat the monsters rather than become one of them. Yet I know he believes, in some dark place inside even I can't touch, that he shares their nature. I know that's why he left.

Jeremiah came back to school before Thanksgiving. He told me that Antoine went to Oklahoma, where most of the descendants of the Natchez nation live now. He's gone in search of something that will put a final end to the deadly vampires sleeping beneath my house. I know that Jeremiah blames me for Antoine leaving. He avoids me, though he and Connor have become quite good friends. Once, in class, when Mr. Corbin called me Harper Ellory, I caught Jeremiah staring at the ring on my finger. He gave me a sad smile that broke my heart.

I wish we were still friends. I wish I had someone, anyone, to talk to.

I thought I felt alone when first we came here. Since Antoine left, though, I'm alone in a different way. A hard way. Antoine isn't dead—well, he is, I guess, but he is still present in the world. He may as well be dead to me, though. I've started to call him a hundred times, but my finger hovers over the phone, then slides away. I know he isn't coming back. I saw it in his face that night by the tunnels, when he compelled Connor to forget everything he'd seen. When I remember the way Connor looked that night, how ready my brother was to walk away from the restoration grant he worked so hard to get just to keep me safe, I know it was the right thing to do. I can't be the one to take away Connor's dream, any more than he could follow it if he thought I was in danger. But I didn't know that staying here without Antoine would feel like this, as if I'm in limbo, with the only person capable of pulling me out of it as profoundly gone as if he has never been.

Connor can't know I married a vampire to save us from danger. And I'm guessing he wouldn't see it that way if he did know. So the marriage certificate stays in the box beneath the bed, and I wear a three-century-old emerald worth more than the house to school every day.

I know I should take it off.

But I just can't, Tessa.

Happy Thanksgiving, I guess, wherever you are.

YOUR TWIN,
Harper

CHAPTER 1

GARDEN

"*D*id you know it's my birthday next month?" Avery is swinging her legs off the end of the dock. I'm painting. The air smells of newly turned earth from the garden I've been digging just behind us.

"It would be difficult to forget." Cass speaks without looking up from her book, her tone gently teasing. "Considering you mention it on a daily basis." She is sitting on the wooden boards with her legs stretched out, her back against a post.

"Well, it's important. I am sixteen, going on seventeen." Avery stands up as she sings the words and does an exaggerated twirl. "But unlike Liesl in *The Sound of Music*, I do *not* need somebody older and wiser telling me what to do." She turns to me. "Which is why I was hoping you'd say yes to me having my party here." She gives me her best doe-eyed, pleading look. "That way we can celebrate with no parentals. And besides, this place is awesome." Avery is so impossibly beautiful that even I find it difficult to say no to the wide brown eyes and tragic face. But then I imagine a mansion full of drunk, hormonal teenagers dancing right above the two starving vampires in our cellar and steel myself to refuse.

"It's not really my decision." I do my best to look apologetic. "Connor isn't much of a party person, and the mansion is his project. I doubt he'll want to risk damaging anything."

"Leave Connor to me." Avery leaps to her feet and marches toward the house with more alacrity than strictly necessary.

I sigh. "Connor doesn't have a chance, does he?"

"Nope." Cass smiles at me. She has a peaceful, quiet presence and often comes down to the dock to read a book while I'm painting or gardening. When I first knew her, I thought her sense of humor was a little sharp, her one liners a touch snarky. Time, though, has made me realise the snark is definitely more an Avery thing. Cass sometimes affects it, but this, I've learned, is more of a façade she adopts to protect herself, to mask her true nature. In reality she is one of the most gentle people I know. When we're alone, she lets the mask drop, and the smart comments with it. I suspect that the edgy sense of humor is down to her lifelong friendship with Avery, who at times can have a sharp tongue indeed. Cass is compassionate and kind, which is probably why Avery and she have remained close for so long. Underneath her exterior, Avery is deeply insecure. She needs friends like Cass who don't compete with her, who offer a gentle place to land when she screws up – which Avery definitely has an ability to do.

I normally hate people watching me work. Cass's presence, though, is soothing. And since Antoine left, I'm in no position to reject company. Sometimes I think about telling Cass everything that happened. If anyone might understand, I think it would be her. But I know I can't. Even if she didn't think I was completely insane, it isn't fair to drag anyone else into this.

"Come on." I take down my canvas and unscrew the easel. "We should go up and rescue Connor."

"Are you sure Connor wants to be rescued?" Cass shoots me a sideways look. "Avery is the kind of girl that every boy dreams about, and she's been spending every waking minute here for weeks."

I want to tell Cass that going by the way Connor looks at her when he thinks nobody is watching, it isn't Avery he's dreaming about, but I figure that would only make things weird. I say instead, "Avery isn't really Connor's type," and leave it there.

The sound of Avery's laughter trickles through the back door. She and Connor are in the kitchen. I leave my easel propped up against the wall and follow Cass through in time to hear Avery say, "But if we promise to stay out of the library, you'll say yes? Everyone will be outside, anyways. I was thinking a fire by the river and fairy lights throughout the garden." She turns to me, her eyes sparkling. "Connor's cool with it," she beams.

I give Connor a questioning look over her shoulder, and he raises his hands in a gesture of half apology, half surrender.

I swallow my inner dread. "Sounds like you've got it all planned." I put on my best attempt at a smile. "How many people are you thinking?"

"That's the best part." Avery can barely contain her excitement. "Your place is huge. The police never come out this way, and you don't have any close neighbors to complain about the noise. I figure we can invite our whole class without any trouble. But it will take me time to set it all up. You're going to be seeing a lot of me in the next few weeks." The look she gives Connor is enough to sear the paint from the walls. Connor glances sideways at Cass then awkwardly down at the ground. He mumbles something about getting tools from his truck and makes a fast exit. I wince inwardly at Avery's look of disappointment as she watches him go. I suspect Avery has never had to put in a moment's effort with a man before. Connor's rejection has triggered the insecurity lying just under her carefully maintained surface. Cass is right about Avery spending every waking minute here. Barely a day goes by without her finding some excuse to come by. I love Avery, and I treasure her friendship. But I'm not entirely comfortable with the direction in which she and Connor seem headed, for either of them.

"Are you really sure you want to have your party here?" I gesture at the cracked plaster and peeling walls, the exposed wires hanging from the ceiling. "We barely have one functional bathroom, and trust me, those pipes are not at all reliable."

"And what's a party without drunk girls lining up for the bathroom? Epic love stories start that way." Avery tosses her hair and holds up a remonstrative finger. "You are not getting out of this party, Harper Ellory, no matter what you say."

I try not to wince when she says my name. Every time someone calls me by Ellory, I think of the marriage certificate hidden under my bed and feel like a fraud.

But I'm not really married, I remind myself, something I also do every time this happens. *And it isn't like I've seen my husband since our wedding day.*

That thought makes me feel inexpressibly lonely. I look up to find Cass watching me. Avery has gone back to planning where she will put people and food and is still talking as if we are listening.

"That ring you wear." Cass speaks quietly enough that only I hear her. "I heard you tell Avery it's a family heirloom." I nod, dropping my head so she can't see the lie in my eyes. "It's strange." I can feel her eyes on me. "I just don't remember you wearing it when you first came here. But now I never see you without it."

"I only found it again recently." I avoid her eyes.

"I haven't seen that sexy uncle of Jeremiah's around in a while." She's still watching me.

"No. I think he's left town." I summon up a bright smile. "I can't hear Avery talking, which is actually scarier than when she won't stop. Shall we go and find her?"

CHAPTER 2

SECRETS

*W*hen my phone dings the following night with a text message, I'm expecting yet another idea from Avery about her party. I see Antoine's name on the screen instead, and my heart screeches to a halt, then starts thudding again, so loud I can hear it. I stare at the name for a long time before I slide the message open. *Have found Natchez woman who knows history of seal. Her name is Noya. She will come to house to see you. Trying to find how to free you from binding. Antoine.*

Trying to find how to free you from binding.

I feel a lurch of disappointment then immediately feel stupid. Of course, he is trying to find a way around the binding. Or a way to actually kill what is sleeping in the cellar below. I knew that was what he had gone in search of. But a secret part of me wonders what it is he truly wants to free me from—the binding, or marriage to him?

I should want to be free of the marriage, I guess. It's not like getting married at seventeen is anyone's life goal.

But I don't. And it hurts more than I like to admit that Antoine seems so intent on finding a way out of it.

I twist the comforting weight of the emerald on my finger. *Always.* I remember the way he looked at me when he said that word, and how it made me feel, as if we were bound in a way nothing could ever break. Now it seems he wants nothing more than to free himself of anything that binds us together. I have a thousand unanswered questions and no way to ask them.

I wander downstairs and find Connor whistling tunelessly as he sands a wall in one of the state rooms. I take up position beside him and we work together for a while in comfortable silence. The dusk is filled with a chorus of bird call, the haunting sounds of the mourning doves that nest in the roof, the woodpeckers in the gnarled live oak beyond the window. They trill the air in such a mass of chatter it makes Connor look at me and laugh. "Do you think they're talking about us?"

"I doubt we're that interesting."

"You're probably right." Connor takes a pull on his beer. "I was thinking that perhaps you could paint a mural in here. On this wall. If you wanted to."

"Really?" I look at the vast expanse, already excited by what I might create. "Wouldn't that impact the restoration grant?"

"The grant covers the structure, not decoration. So long as you aren't knocking walls down, feel free to paint anything you like." He smiles. "Now, if only you looked that enthusiastic about your math homework."

"I'm never going to be excited about math homework. But this—I can't wait to get started."

"I'm glad." Connor turns back to his sanding. "You seemed like you needed something to cheer you up. You don't seem to go out much anymore." I think of the last party I went to, when Antoine compelled a pack of men from the bayou to dance naked on the road after they attacked me, and stifle a smile. "I'm happy here." It's the truth. In reality I've never wanted to do anything other than paint and garden, anyway. I have no idea how I'm going to make a living out of either, but somehow I know I was put on this earth to do both, and so there is almost nothing in the world that could make me happier than a blank wall and paint to make it come alive and bare earth out back in which to plant.

Almost nothing.

I remember Antoine's message and turn away so Connor can't see my face. "I forgot to tell you." I strive for as casual a tone as I can manage. "I was making some enquiries at Cass's mom's shop about the supposed curse on our mansion. Selena put me in touch with a woman, Noya, from the Natchez nation up in Oklahoma. Noya apparently has an interest in alternative history. Magic, curses, that kind of thing. She's going to be in Deepwater soon and wants to come and have a look around. I said it was fine. I hope that's okay?"

"Sure thing." Connor shrugs. Then, in a studiedly casual voice to rival my own, he says, "What shop is it that Cass's mom has, again?"

My face is still hidden, so he doesn't see my smile. "It's called Witch Way. Kind of a hippy shop. But there are some really interesting artifacts and books in there and a display of old jewelry. You're such a history nerd that you'd probably like it." I wait a beat. "Cass works there in the afternoons after school to give her mom a break."

"That's nice of her." Connor is going for a neutral tone, but I can see the faint tinge of color at the neck of his T-shirt.

"Cass is a nice girl." Now I'm really stirring the pot, but I can't help it. Cass *is* a nice girl. And if anyone needs a nice girl, it's my brother. Connor is ridiculously good-looking. He's also completely unaware of it and a genuinely kind person. As a result, he's always been a magnet for girls with insecurity issues. Avery, for all her stunning good looks, is classic Connor kryptonite. He doesn't have the heart to tell her outright that he isn't interested, and the longer it goes on, the more he will find himself stuck in something he doesn't want, all because he doesn't quite have the courage to approach the girl he actually wants.

He clears his throat and takes another swallow of his beer. I take pity on him and change the subject. "How are we going to manage this party of Avery's?"

Connor shakes his head and rolls his eyes skyward as he sands. "Truly, I don't know. The place is a health and safety nightmare. I'll have to put barricades up everywhere and lock what doors we can."

"Especially the library." I try to keep my tone light, but it's been worrying me ever since Avery came up with the idea. "I think we should put a lock on that door and make sure people know it is out of bounds. If anyone accidentally opens that hidden passageway, we could find ourselves with a drunk accident on those dark stairs."

"Of course." Connor frowned. "Maybe I should go down there and take a look. You know, I'd actually forgotten about that staircase. And the cellar." Too late, I remember Antoine compelling Connor to do exactly that.

"I don't think there's any need to go that far," I say hastily. "You said it's dangerous, remember? Maybe just lock the door to keep others out." Connor nods, but there is a faint crease between his brows, as if he's trying to remember something. I curse my own stupidity. I know my brother too well. He's unlikely to forget about the staircase again, not without Antoine there to make sure he does. And Antoine isn't here.

It always comes back to that.

"I'm working on a house close to town tomorrow. How about I drive you to school and pick you up?" Connor turns away to sand a doorframe. His voice has that same super casual note that red-flags exactly how much he doesn't want me to notice what he's actually saying. "Maybe we could go to that witch shop on the way home. There might be some things in there worth a look."

"Sure." I smile behind his back. "Why not?"

We sand on in companionable silence, the chorus of bird-song giving way to the lonely, distant caw of a nighthawk.

CHAPTER 3

NATCHEZ

*T*he next day when Connor drops me off at school, Jeremiah is talking to Avery in the parking lot. She breaks off the conversation and rushes over as soon as she spots us. Connor sighs audibly but smiles like the nice guy he is. Jeremiah's face falls as he watches Avery make a beeline for Connor. I shoot him a sympathetic smile, but when he sees me watching him, his expression hardens and he turns away.

I'm still not forgiven, then.

Avery is chatting away about arrangements for the party, pushing a reluctant Connor to make a time to meet. The sister in me really wants to mention going to Cass's shop this afternoon, just to force Connor to confront the triangle I see closing in around him, but my inner sadist proves unequal to creating such havoc. In the end, I watch with some exasperation as Connor grudgingly agrees to be home on the weekend, and Avery begins planning what she is going to bring along and what jobs need to be done. I take it from the long list that I'm likely to have a house guest all weekend. I don't mind, if I'm honest. I know Avery comes to drool over Connor, but she truly does have a beautiful heart, and I like having her around, even though I know it isn't ideal for Connor.

"I'll see you this afternoon," I mouth to Connor behind Avery's back as we head into school. He gestures frantically at the exit to the lot, and I understand he means he will meet me outside the gates. I shake my head in mock remonstration and he rolls his eyes as he pulls out in his truck. I'm still grinning when I turn to go inside and actually walk right into Jeremiah.

"Sorry," I say awkwardly. "I didn't do that on purpose." For a moment I think he's going to just ignore me, then his face softens a little, and he ducks his head. "I know." He gives me a small smile. "How are you, Harper?"

I half shrug and don't answer. "How are you?" I ask instead. "I've been out to see you a couple of times, but you're not home a lot." *Or you're not answering the door for me,* I think, but don't say.

"I've been doing some work for your brother after school and on the weekends."

"Sure. Connor mentioned you were." Actually, he hasn't, and I'm suddenly tempted to invite Avery along this afternoon just to annoy him.

"I need to talk to you." Jeremiah looks around the corridor and lowers his voice. "I heard from Antoine last night. He's sending someone down to look at the mansion." I'm about to say that he sent me the same message, but then I see the light in Jeremiah's eyes, and realize that hearing from Antoine might well be the highlight of his week. I don't want to diminish his delight, so I don't say anything except to thank him for letting me know. "I was thinking that maybe I might come over when this Noya lady does," he goes on, his eyes shifting to me then away again, as if he's not sure what I will say to that.

"I think that's a great idea." I try not to show how happy I am. "Connor might appreciate some help around the place, too, if you've got spare time. We've got a lot to organize before this party of Avery's."

"Will Avery be there this weekend? Noya's related to her, you know. Some distant Natchez connection. It might be good for them to meet. And maybe I can help take some of the work for the party off Connor's shoulders." He does an even worse job than Connor does of hiding his interest. I pretend not to notice.

"Yes, Avery's planning to stay all weekend, from what I can gather." Mentally I'm changing the Connor, Avery, and Cass triangle to a more complicated shape, one that puts Jeremiah as close to Avery as he can get. It doesn't bode well.

I also can't help wondering about the coincidence of Noya and Avery being related. Somehow I doubt it's coincidence at all. Unfortunately, only one person is likely to be able to answer that question; but digital messages notwithstanding, Antoine is as far away as he has ever been.

"Well, I'll see you this weekend, then." Jeremiah gives me the closest thing resembling a smile that I've had from him since Antoine left. "It's good to talk to you, Harper." I watch him go, torn between happiness that we are on better terms at last, and creeping worry at the thought of the tangled emotional web growing between my brother and my friends. I try to shake it off. Being closer to the one person who knows my secrets makes me feel temporarily less alone. I'm not ready to lose Jeremiah again. I can only hope Avery lets him down gently, rather than with the careless crash I suspect her capable of.

After school I escape the lot without being accosted by Avery, and Connor pulls out immediately. I swear he's actually checking his rearview mirror. "You know," I say conversationally as he heads into town, "it would have served you right if I'd told Avery where you're going this afternoon. I can't believe you didn't tell me Jeremiah was working with you after school."

Connor lifts a shoulder. "Didn't think it mattered. Why? Do

you like him? You went to a party or something with him a while back, I remember."

"Yes. But it's nothing like that. We're just friends, is all." I mentally kick myself. Secrets hold so many traps. I remember sitting by Connor's blood-soaked body with Jeremiah while we waited for Antoine to hunt down Keziah and Caleb. Connor doesn't remember any of it. He has no idea why Jeremiah would be any more than a casual acquaintance.

We pull up in front of Witch Way. Through the window I can see several figures moving around, more customers than I've ever seen at one time. "Looks kind of crowded."

But Connor's eyes are fixed on Cass's tall figure behind the counter. "Couple more won't matter any." He's already opening the door. I try not to smile.

The hanging chimes make a tune as we open the door and step inside. Cass looks up from the counter, and for a moment her face breaks into an unguarded smile, her eyes glowing softly as she looks at Connor. I feel something in my heart shift, for my brother and for Cass.

"Hey," says Connor quietly.

"Hey." Cass smiles, and even a blind man could see that there is nobody else in the room for either of them. I'm moving surreptitiously off to the side to give them some space when Cass turns her smile to me. "It's good timing that you came today. Noya and her nephew, Tate, have come all the way from Oklahoma to have a look at the Marigny mansion. You've just saved me a drive out to introduce them. Noya—this is Connor Ellory and his sister, Harper."

The couple at the desk turn around, and the woman, who is tall and elegant, with long dark hair, jeans, and a boho shirt, puts out her hand. "It's nice to meet you both." She shakes our hands, smiling. "I'm Noya, and this is my nephew, Tate. He's a specialist in the tribal history of this area."

Tate is even taller than his aunt and looks about the same

age as Antoine, early twenties. He's got Noya's sharp, angular features, as well as her long dark hair, tied back at his neck. His smile is as open as Noya's and he takes my hand with genuine interest. "Harper," he says, but he isn't looking at my face. He is staring at the ring on my hand. When he looks back up at me his smile is firmly in place, but I saw it, the moment when his mouth tightened and his eyes narrowed, and so when I answer him I can't quite hide the wariness in my tone.

"Tate." His hand is cool and smooth, but I sense strength in his brief grip. "I didn't realize two people would be coming."

"No." His smile still hasn't wavered, but something lurks behind his eyes. I can see it, and I suspect he knows I can, because there is a wry twist to his mouth when he says, "I was a late addition to the journey. I just came to keep my aunt company. We haven't seen one another in a while."

"Tate has been lecturing in Georgia for a time. It's good to have him home." Noya casts her nephew a warm smile. There is a slight sadness to her face, as if she carries grief somewhere inside. It's an expression I know well. I get the impression she is the kind of person to keep her troubles private, however.

Tate gestures to a cabinet full of jewelry, mostly beaten silver filled with stones like lapis and moonstone. Most of the cabinets are lit, but this one is dark, the pieces clearly less valuable than some of the others. At the back of the rows of silver lies another, dusty row of earrings and pendants carved from wood, bone, and shell. They are crude and clunky, not very attractive. "I notice you have some pendants carved from wood and bone," Tate says to Cass. "Where do you get them?"

"Mom does the ordering. I'm not sure."

"This one suits you." Tate holds up a shell piece with a spiral design. He's right, it does look beautiful next to Cass's skin, and she is clearly a little flustered by the attention and his warm smile. Connor frowns. As if sensing his tension, Tate turns the same warm smile to him. "I saw the proposal you drew for the Marigny mansion." He says the one thing guaranteed to charm my brother, and sure enough, Connor's face immediately relaxes into a self-conscious smile. "It's wonderful." Tate speaks with such obvious sincerity that my initial reserve is rapidly fading. "I lecture in history at the University of Georgia. I'm good friends with one of the members of the Legacy Committee who decided to award you the grant. I know how excited everyone is about your plans. I can't wait to see what you've done." He and Connor instantly fall into a complex discussion about foundations and architecture, of which I understand almost nothing. I'm willing to bet Cass doesn't, either, but her eyes glow as she watches Connor talking animatedly about the mansion, and when he looks up to find her watching him, my brother smiles crookedly and looks so happy that when Tate finally turns to me, I'm all but ready to hug him.

Tate subtly draws Cass into his conversation with Connor by the jewelry cabinet and then extricates himself just as deftly. Connor is actually laughing and talking openly in a way he rarely does with anyone, and Cass seems genuinely fascinated as he tells her about his plans for the mansion. Tate and Noya join me beside the door. Tate nods at Cass and Connor, then winks conspiratorially at me. "It's probably a good time for us to leave."

Noya leans in close to me, speaking low enough to be unheard by Connor or Cass. "I met Avery and her parents earlier when we arrived in town. Avery mentioned she's heading out to see you this weekend. I thought that might be a good time to look at the mansion, if it suits you? I'd like to spend some time with Avery, too. And Jeremiah, of course. Antoine told me a lot about him."

"That sounds good." I smile at them both, fighting the fierce desire to ask what else Antoine might have said. "I'm glad you got in touch with Jeremiah." I try to maintain a cheerful smile. "I think it's important for him to keep a connection to the mansion."

"I imagine he's fascinated by your brother's progress." Tate holds the door open for me. "I gather the mansion was quite the ruin before your brother began the restoration. Jeremiah is fortunate there are grants available—mansions such as those are an expensive business to restore."

I wonder for a moment why he thinks the restoration of the mansion will benefit Jeremiah, but I don't think on it for long. There is something both warm and non-threatening about Tate. I find his presence oddly comforting, like the scent of baked bread in a house.

"I don't think his parents created much of a home," I confide. "Now he's doing really well in school, and he seems to like working with Connor." What I really mean is that the sale of the mansion brought Antoine into Jeremiah's life, a trade I suspect Jeremiah would make again in a heartbeat. I catch the thought before it goes down the inevitable road straight to my heart. "My brother buying the mansion might actually be the best thing that ever happened to Jeremiah."

For the briefest moment, Tate's eyes narrow, and the warm smile falters. It's fleeting, just as it was earlier when he noticed the ring on my finger, but it's there, nonetheless.

"I didn't realize your brother actually bought the mansion." Is it my imagination, or is he looking at me more closely than he did before?

"Yes, we own it." I watch him carefully, but when he nods, he seems entirely unconcerned, and I think I must have imagined his reaction. I sigh inwardly.

That's the problem with secrets, I think later, as Connor and I drive home in companionable silence. *Keeping them makes you think everyone else is doing the same.*

"So Cass is going to come out this weekend, too." Connor casts me a sideways glance as we pull up in front of the house.

I manage to keep a straight face while he's looking at me, but I can't help smiling as I get out of the car.

If I can't have my own romance, I guess I can, at least, live vicariously through my brother's.

CHAPTER 4

FRANKINCENSE

J have fun making the house ready for our pre-party gathering this weekend. I've already begun sketching the mural on the wall, doing some chalk shading to get an idea of perspective. I'm developing a large garden party scene, using live oaks as the frame, as if the viewer is looking down a tunnel through time and distance to what I plan as a period scene, set during the time when the mansion was built. It is a delicate political balance, I know, but I hope to create something sensitive to both reality and current sensibilities.

I spend a lot of time in the garden, too. It's taking shape, almost as if it had a heart and will of its own. Herbs and flowers emerge that I only vaguely recall planting.

I bind large bunches of flowers to place throughout the mansion, using old bottles and whatever else I can find as vases, and do what I can to make the interior seem artistic rather than crumbling. "The cool thing about the whole fading grandeur vibe of this place," says Cass as she helps me arrange mismatching chairs around our old, scarred table, "is that it makes everything in it look artful, even junk." Her eyes cut to where Connor is standing on a ladder mending a light fixture, and I smile to myself at the way her eyes linger on the bare skin between his T-shirt and jeans. At the sound of a motorcycle outside, I leave them to it, well aware that my presence is unlikely to be missed by either party. I've left them alone most of the morning, and it hasn't escaped me that they haven't spent a moment of that time apart.

Jeremiah parks and takes off his helmet, frowning when he sees only Cass's car beside mine and Connor's. "I thought Avery was coming." He looks disappointed. I hide another smile.

"She is." I managed to delay Avery's arrival until midday, on the pretext that Connor has some technical work to do on the house for which he needs space. I know it was sneaky, but I also know that with Avery present, Cass and Connor would have had no chance at a private discussion.

"We need to get Connor and Cass out of the house for a while." Jeremiah lowers his voice. "So that Noya and Tate can have a look at the cellar."

"Tate?" I frown. "I thought he was just Noya's nephew."

"He's a historian, Harper. He's also Natchez." He shrugs. "He may not know the details, but Noya wouldn't have brought him along if he had nothing to offer."

"Well, I guess, when you put it like that." I'm still unconvinced. "If that's the case though, it seems a bit odd that he didn't know about me owning the house."

Jeremiah frowns. "He should. Noya knows most of the story, as far as I know. The whole reason she's here is to try to find a way to separate you from the binding."

"Well, she clearly didn't tell Tate." I tell him about Tate's comments in the shop. "He seemed to recognize my ring, as well. Doesn't that seem strange to you?"

"Some, I guess. But like I said—he's a historian, not an occultist like Noya. I figure Antoine told Noya to keep the details quiet." He gives me a meaningful look. "Wouldn't you?"

It's a good point. Having an interest in history and tribal curses, is one thing. Vampires in the cellar are quite another.

"Why don't I ask Connor to show Cass and Avery how he's planning to set up by the river?" Jeremiah suggests. "I'll make sure Tate goes with them and that they don't hurry back. That should give you enough time to show Noya the cellar." I'm nodding when Avery's car pulls into the drive, closely followed by a rental I assume belongs to Noya. There is a clatter of car doors and cheerful banter, and suddenly the house seems full, as if it has been waiting for laughter to bring it alive.

"Come on in and put it on the table." I eye the large picnic basket in Tate's hand. "You didn't need to bring all this," I add as he follows me in, throwing a bag toward Connor as he does.

"But I'm glad you did," grins Connor, catching the bag and extracting a six-pack of beer dewy with cold. He opens one for himself and another for Tate, putting the rest in the icebox. "It's past midday, isn't it?" he calls through the window. "That makes it beer thirty, Mississippi time." I roll my eyes and Tate winks at me as he heads out and settles in beside Connor, taking the proffered beer. They clink bottles and immediately launch into a discussion of plans and angles completely unfathomable to the rest of us.

Avery pulls a face, clearly put out at being so quickly cut out of the conversation. "I'm going to organize my party," she announces, wandering off toward the back porch. "Cass, why don't you and Jeremiah fetch those fairy lights from my car? I'll show you where I want them hung." Jeremiah is pink with pleasure at being singled out. Cass rolls her eyes at Avery's imperious tone but throws me a conspiratorial smile and follows Jeremiah.

Noya turns to me, her face sobering. "I feel it," she says quietly, under cover of the others' chatter. "The magic here. It's heavy on the air."

I nod. I know what she means. "How much did Antoine tell you?"

"He said a binding was placed on the deed to the mansion long ago, to hold dark spirits in the cellar here. A blood link forged between Natchez, slaves, and the Marigny family, He told me he is trying to find a way to separate the binding from the Marigny name, to split the magic holding the spirits from the deed itself."

I feel a strange thickness in my chest. Antoine is trying to free me, to undo what binds him and I. If there is no need for my name on that deed, there is no need for us to be married.

Antoine has clearly decided that we cannot be together. I shouldn't be surprised. He said it plain enough, after all. But though my logical mind knew it, heard him say it, something inside me hasn't accepted it until this moment, and it hurts.

Noya is looking closely at me. "You didn't know he was trying to break the binding?"

I shake my head and swallow, turning away so she can't see my face. "I did," I say unevenly. "I guess I just didn't realize he'd act so quickly."

"I understand the deed is in your name." There is so much understanding in her voice that I can't look at her. I nod. "Then you understand how important it is that we do this carefully," she says.

"Yes." I take a breath and compose myself before I look at her. "Nobody but Jeremiah knows the truth. Not my brother, or my friends. I want it kept that way. Did Antoine tell you"—I choose my words carefully—"what exactly lies in the cellar?" Noya meets my eyes and nods slowly.

"It wasn't entirely new to me. The story has been handed down in my family." She looks at me closely. "I take it from your question that you know what is down there, too."

"I know it all. And Tate, your nephew?"

She shakes her head. "Some. Not all. He knows the basic

story of the curse, but I imagine he thinks it no more than fantasy. He doesn't know any of the details. His knowledge of Natchez history, though, is second to none. We may well need that kind of help." I nod. I'd thought as much.

There is the sound of footsteps as she speaks, and Jeremiah comes into the room. "The others have gone down to the river. You're clear, for a while at least."

I show Noya through to the library. The bookshelf that guards the stairway down to the cellar is already slightly ajar.

I turn to Jeremiah. "Did you open it?" He shakes his head. I frown. Connor must have followed up on his thought to check on it, which worries me.

Noya shivers as I push the bookshelf properly open. "The presence here is strong. Whatever is down there is definitely awake."

She starts down the stairs and Jeremiah holds me back, giving me a warning look. He waits until Noya is out of earshot and whispers, "Something isn't right."

"What do you mean?"

"Tate." Jeremiah's face is grave. "I'm about certain he just tried to compel me."

"What? How? What did he say?" I think back to Tate's face, his manner, but there isn't anything there to make me think he's a vampire.

Then again, I hadn't suspected Antoine, either.

"On the way to the river he held back, let the others walk ahead. Then he looked me right in the eye and asked me whose name was on the deed to the mansion. It was the way he asked it, Harper. I've seen Antoine compel people before. He had the same look in his eyes—intent, as if he expected me to answer. But I chew a little raw frankincense every morning now, and I carry it with me everywhere." He reaches into his pocket and pulls out a gnarled, golden lump. It's opaque and looks a little like tree sap, it's scent rich on the afternoon air. "Frankincense is toxic to vampires. It prevents compulsion. Antoine said the raw stuff works best, though incense sticks can, too, so long as it's made from real frankincense. He gave me a large jar of it and told me to burn it in the house and to chew it myself. I never go anywhere without it, now." He looks momentarily self-conscious. "I don't burn it in the house, though. If I did . . ." his voice trails off. I don't need him to finish the sentence. If he burns it in the house, it would mean Antoine couldn't enter.

Antoine never mentioned frankincense to me. My logical mind says there seems to be little point in my using frankin-cense to prevent compulsion if I can't be compelled anyway, but my heart doesn't care much for logic. I push away the familiar rabbit hole of hurt and add the question of why he wouldn't share such information with me to the ever-growing pile of unanswered questions, and I try instead to focus on what Jere-miah is saying.

"What did you do when Tate asked you that? How did you react?"

"I told him I wasn't too sure on the details or whose name was on the deed. I told him that I just signed where Antoine told me. I thought it was better to pretend I was compelled, and that I didn't know anything." He looks at me anxiously. "Was that the right thing to do?"

"I think so." I try to think it through. My relief that Jeremiah and I are finally talking again is overshadowed by the reasons we're doing so.

More secrets.

I wish Jeremiah weren't caught up in all this.

"Are you absolutely sure Tate was compelling you, Jeremiah? Maybe he was just asking the question."

"Maybe." Jeremiah looks unconvinced. "But I don't think so. It was weird, Harper. The way he was looking at me. I just think there's something not quite right about him."

From down the stairs, Noya calls out to me.

"Coming!" I call back. "Let's just wait and see," I say to Jeremiah. "And maybe not say anything to Antoine just yet. I don't want to alarm him."

"Antoine would want to know," Jeremiah says quietly. "Especially if you're in danger, Harper."

I think of Antoine going all the way to Oklahoma, trying everything he can to break the one binding that holds us together. "I don't want Antoine running back here to rescue me." My tone is forceful enough to make Jeremiah's eyes widen slightly. "We'll manage this between ourselves for now, Jeremiah. Okay?"

He tilts his head in a neutral gesture. "I still think you should call him."

"Well, that isn't going to happen."

Noya calls to me again, but as I start down the stairs, Tate comes into the room. "I think I'm better served here than party planning." He's so cheerful, so human and nonthreatening, that I honestly wonder if Jeremiah has imagined the entire thing.

Tate heads down the stairs ahead of me and behind his back, I look questioningly at Jeremiah. He spreads his hands in a "not much I can do" gesture. I shrug.

I guess we don't have a choice.

I follow Tate down the stairs.

CHAPTER 5

HEIRLOOMS

*I*t's the first time I've been in the stairwell since the cellar was resealed. I forgot how still and silent it is, as if the air itself waits for what is behind the door to stir. Noya takes the stairs slowly, seeming almost to wince with each step. "Old age." She shoots me an apologetic glance. "Not quite so agile as I once was." Since she looks barely over forty, I suspect it's the magic in the air rather than the exertion that's slowing her down. At the bottom, she touches the symbol on the door and shivers. "Do you recognize this?" she asks Tate.

He steps closer. His expression is guarded, as if he's exerting some effort to appear calm. "It's the symbol of the Natchez treaty with the French." On the surface his tone holds only detached, professional interest, but when he touches the totem, I notice that his hand shakes slightly. "It's a potent symbol," he says quietly. "One that is said to have involved great sacrifice."

"That's the problem." Noya frowns as she traces it. "The blood given to create this totem, and the magic it binds, was taken not only from the Natchez, but from the magician who helped them, and from the Marigny family themselves. To release it will take the same combination in equal measure." She looks at Tate apologetically. "I realize the magic part is not really your area. I hadn't meant to involve you in anything other than the symbolism."

"To the contrary." Again, Tate's tone is calm, but there's an unmistakeable tension in his jaw that belies his easy manner. "Symbolism is magic, at its core. Ask any computer programmer." He smiles, but his eyes are serious. "I'm here to help," he says. "Perhaps my knowledge of history may be of use, even if my occult skills are lacking."

Noya smiles at him and turns to me. "We would need descendants of those original workers of the binding," she says. "The totem itself belongs to my people, so I can help with the Natchez blood. I know the forces of the earth here. I can feel them, work with them. But I can't weave the magic that combines the seal with the binding itself. I know nothing of the blood magic that created the binding, nor how to separate it from this house or this land."

"That's the reason the Natchez involved the slaves." Tate's voice is unexpectedly harsh. Seeing our surprise, he immediately alters it, his handsome face softening. "I've read much of the history of this area. It still makes me angry, even if the stories are long past. There was a time when the only forces at play on this land came from the earth itself and my people's ability to work with it." He shakes his head. "But with white men came first their magic, then that of the slaves they brought with them. Such things change a land. In only a few years—this." He gestures to the door, his face dark. "I do not fully understand what it is you believe lies behind this door, Aunt," he says to Noya, "but I'm Natchez, too. I know our stories as well as I do the pages of history books. And even if I didn't, I would still feel the presence in that cellar."

His eyes on me are questioning, but I avoid answering. There's no need for anyone to know more than is necessary.

"Cass and her mother, Selena, are descended from Samuel,

the slave who made the binding," I say. "Jeremiah is a direct descendant of the original Marignys. And Avery is Natchez and a descendant of the medicine woman, Atsila, just as you are. Would that be enough, do you think, for the magic to work?"

Before Noya can answer, Tate interrupts. "Atsila." Even in the dim light of the stairwell, I can tell his face is ashen. "How do you know that name?"

"I must have seen it written somewhere when I was researching the curse." Instinct warns me against sharing too much with Tate, particularly after what Jeremiah told me.

"No," Tate says slowly, staring at me. "It isn't written anywhere. Very few of our own people even know that name."

"Oh." I shrug, as if I haven't noticed his reaction, and turn back to Noya, hoping he can't tell how on edge I feel. "So, do you think it would help if you worked with Selena and Avery?"

Noya shakes her head, thankfully too absorbed in studying the symbol to have noticed the exchange between Tate and I. "I've met Selena. And though I like her and Cass a great deal, neither of them has the skill to rework this binding."

"Can't you teach them?" I ask.

"Like I said—I don't know what magic was used. It was foreign to our people then, and it still is now." Noya lays her hand over the totem, her eyes closed. A dull thud cuts the silence, as if the air itself stirs. Jeremiah shudders beside me. I shiver, feeling the familiar, unsettling chill as the air grows colder. Tate is very still, watching Noya closely, his face carefully blank. Eventually she sighs and opens her eyes.

"They know we're here." Realizing what she's said, Noya colors and glances guiltily at Tate.

"Are the stories true, then?" he asks quietly. "Are there really bodies in that cellar?" Noya nods cautiously.

Is it just my imagination, or are those wide eyes of his just a little too practiced, his expression of surprise just a touch too carefully contrived? I notice Jeremiah watching Tate with the same skepticism. *So, not only my imagination, then.*

"Like I said, I'm Natchez too." Tate seems to have recovered his composure after his earlier surprise, though I still see a shadow behind his eyes when he looks at me. "I know the legends, and I've heard the stories. I guess I just didn't think they were true." He gives us a rueful smile. "You have to admit, cursed corpses seem a little far-fetched."

Cursed corpses. *He didn't say the word.* I don't dare meet Jeremiah's eyes. When it becomes apparent none of us intends to actually speak, Tate continues. "If what I understand is correct, we would also need the person whose name is bound to the deed of the mansion itself. Is that your brother, Harper?" His tone is deceptively casual, but I'm not the only one unsettled by his question.

"I've spoken to the owner." Noya's watching Tate with a faint crease of suspicion between her brows. "They wish to remain anonymous, but if we need help, they will give us what we need."

"Good." Tate nods, casual and unconcerned again. "Though I have no idea where we might start, Aunt. Do you?" He is studying the totem on the door again with that same air of detachment, but I'm not at all sure his interest is academic, and looking at Noya's watchful expression, I suspect she's begun to question the coincidence of her nephew turning up just as she was coming here. Tate, I'm increasingly certain, isn't here by accident. That begs the question—why *is* he here?

I glance at him surreptitiously. Could Jeremiah be right in thinking he was being compelled earlier? Surely Noya would know if her nephew was a vampire? Looking at his calm, friendly face, I'm momentarily annoyed that I live in a world of such paranoia. Tate is Natchez, after all. Perhaps he is just curious about his own heritage. *Especially when it involves stories of cursed corpses*, I think wryly. I guess anyone might find themselves intrigued by something that crazy. Especially a historian.

"I need to do a little more research." Noya turns away from the door. "Talk with people who know more than I do. I'll come back to you in a few days, after I've had a chance to find out what I can. Jeremiah, can I ask you some questions?" They head up the stairs, Jeremiah giving me a warning glance over his shoulder as he goes, his eyes lingering suspiciously on Tate. I turn to follow them but Tate's voice stops me. "Harper. That ring you wear." His eyes drop to my hand. "Can I ask where it came from?"

"Why?" I counter, holding his eyes. I can't read anything in them but curiosity. There is no flare of surprise at my question, nothing to indicate he has tried to compel me and expects me to answer. If anything, he looks slightly shamefaced. "There is very little left of my family's heritage. Our history is not one recorded in books. But odd things remain—like this." He holds up a photocopy of an old sketch, done in faded pencil. It is portrait of a woman, with a remarkably beautiful, vaguely familiar face, her hands folded before her. On her left ring finger sits the Marigny emerald, clear and unmistakeable.

"This drawing has been in my family for generations," Tate says, watching me. "I don't know who the woman is, or why we have a picture of her, but when I saw your ring, I recognized it instantly. I had a copy of the sketch sent through to be certain." He nods at it. "Is there anything—anything at all—that you might be able to tell me about that ring? Is it connected somehow to the curse here?" He smiles crookedly. "I promise you, Harper, I've studied things stranger than anything you could imagine. Nothing can surprise me."

His face is so earnest, his yearning for truth so transparent, that for a moment I am tempted to tell him everything. Then I remember the cold, dangerous presence beyond the door and think of how many centuries Antoine has kept his secret.

It's not mine to tell, I think. Regardless of the fact that my name is on the deed, the secrets of the Marigny mansion belong to Antoine and his family. I won't be the one to betray them, nor to put my brother's future in jeopardy.

"I wish I could tell you more." I meet Tate's eyes evenly. "The ring is a family heirloom. I inherited it, but I know nothing of its history. And as for the so-called curse, I truly don't know much about it at all, except that Jeremiah and his uncle believe it could place us in danger. Connor knows hardly anything of it, and I don't want to worry him, which is why I'm a little secretive about what you guys are doing here. He'd be upset if he thought there was any real danger. I'd appreciate it if you kept him out of it."

I'm not lying, exactly. But nor am I telling the truth, and I feel almost certain that Tate knows it.

Tate steps back, his face carefully neutral. "Of course," he says lightly. He glances at my hand. "Maybe the ring is just a coincidence."

"Probably." I gesture to the stairs. "We better go back up, before Connor wonders what we're doing down here."

"Sure." Tate smiles and follows me. I turn away, but I seem to feel his eyes on my back as I climb the stairs, and throughout the long afternoon of Avery's cheerful chatter and party planning, I watch him closely. Tate does nothing at all to rouse suspicion and instead charms Connor so thoroughly that by the end of the day, they are joking like long-lost brothers. Nonetheless, as I watch Noya and Tate drive away later that afternoon, I can't shake a feeling of unease.

I sit in my room late that night, arms around my legs, staring at the moonflowers slowly unfurling from the vine at my window.

I need to talk. To ask advice.

I need Antoine. Without him, none of this makes any sense. Not even Connor's restoration dreams seem important when I weigh them against the cold death lying in the cellar beneath me.

I stare at my phone, willing it to ring. But it doesn't, and although every fiber of my being longs to dial his number, I can't bring myself to do it.

Marrying him was my decision. My choice. Now I am a Marigny, for better or worse.

I must learn to live with it.

Alone, if I must.

The pale moonflowers open, revealing the deep indigo hidden at their core, their fragrance filling the still night.

CHAPTER 6

RETURN

"*P*lease don't be angry." Jeremiah watches me warily in the parking lot before school.

"Why?" I look at him narrowly. "What did you do?"

"Sent Antoine a message."

I stare at him. "Saying what, exactly?"

Jeremiah holds up a hand. "I thought he should know about Tate being here. And I was right. Antoine didn't know anything about Tate coming. He wasn't happy about it, either."

Curiosity gets the better of me. "What did he say?"

"That he'd be home as soon as he could."

"Antoine is coming here?" My heart thuds so heavily I'm momentarily breathless, and when Jeremiah meets my eyes, I see my eagerness mirrored in his own. He nods. I look away, embarrassed that I'm so transparent.

"You shouldn't have messaged him," I mutter without any conviction.

"I don't trust him, Harper. Tate, that is."

"You don't still think he tried to compel you?"

"I don't know." Jeremiah shrugs. "But there's something weird about him. Noya is planning to go back to Oklahoma soon, to talk to some people about the totem, but Tate is staying. Why would he stay?"

I cast him a skeptical look. "Are you sure you aren't just looking for an excuse to get Antoine back home?"

The color mounts in Jeremiah's cheeks, but he doesn't look away. "Are you going to pretend you wish I hadn't asked him to come?"

Now it's my turn to look away. The bell rings.

"You know I'm right," he calls after me as I walk toward my next class. I spend the rest of the day in a state of nervous tension, and when the final bell rings, I emerge from school half expecting to see Antoine's tall, lean figure waiting for me. I see Connor's instead. I don't know if I'm relieved or disappointed.

"Connor!" Avery waves eagerly, and, watched by half of the student body, almost runs toward Connor's truck. I wince. My brother is looking not at Avery, but at Cass's quiet figure a pace behind her, though it is clear the distinction has been lost on Avery. Cass hangs back, clearly unsure of what to do, and Connor looks excruciatingly embarrassed as Avery throws her arms about his neck in an ostentatious display of familiarity.

"Awkward," mutters Jeremiah beside me.

Connor extricates himself from Avery's embrace and takes a hasty step backward. "Did Harper tell you I was coming out tonight to make sure everything is ready for the party tomorrow?" Avery says, already opening the door to his truck. "It's so nice of you to come and pick me up!"

Connor shoots me an agonized glance, and I'm about to intervene when a calm voice speaks up from behind me. "Actually, Avery, I was hoping you might join me instead of Connor." Tate is leaning against a sleek convertible that looks even more expensive than the rental he arrived in the other day. Dressed in a loose linen shirt and trousers, long dark hair tousled, and showing just enough chiselled, tanned chest to send a nearby group of girls into a fit of nervous laughter, he is the kind of bait Avery cannot possibly resist.

"You don't mind, Connor, do you?" Casting my brother a flirtatious look from under her lashes, Avery seems not to notice Connor's visible relief as she turns toward Tate.

"Jeremiah said he is heading on out to the Marigny mansion to check the grounds for any hazards before the party." Tate gives me the ghost of a wink over Avery's head. "I thought I'd tag along. Sometimes there are old artefacts just lying about on ground like yours." He turns to Avery, not waiting for Jeremiah's response. "But I admit I was hoping you'd be there, Avery. Jeremiah, you don't mind riding with Harper, do you?"

Jeremiah exchanges a startled glance with me, but then he looks at Avery's flushed face, and his face twists into a reluctant smile. "Not at all." Tate is back to his impossibly charming self, and despite his earlier suspicions, Jeremiah clearly can't help admiring him. "He's smooth," he murmurs as he gets into the car beside me. Cass is climbing into Connor's truck, and I smile to myself when I see Connor wait until she is inside to close the door behind her and walk around to the driver's side.

"Still think Tate is the bad guy?" I ask as I pull out of the lot.

Jeremiah shrugs and looks sideways at me. "If him being here brings Antoine back, I don't care what he is."

I could argue, but we both know I'd be lying. "Do you know when Antoine will get here?" I ask instead. Jeremiah shakes his head. "He was in Oklahoma when I called, so I'd guess we have a little while."

I try to calm my nerves all the way home, but my stomach is still jittery when we get there. Tate's convertible is parked under the trees. Connor's truck is nowhere to be seen. I grin to myself. I'm guessing Connor has taken Cass somewhere far away from wherever Avery might be.

Avery is fussing over the fairy lights out back, tying lanterns to the trees, and ordering Tate about. "I need to get back to town before the shops close," she calls to me. "I still have some things to pick up."

"Why don't you take my car now," Tate offers, "and buy what you need for the party? I can use the time to have a look around here, then drive you home when you get back."

"Your convertible? Really?" She gives him the benefit of her most dazzling smile. "Aren't you sweet. Thank you."

"That was a nice thing you did." I smile at him as Avery drives away. "At school today, too. You saved Avery from looking foolish and my brother from having to blatantly reject her."

Tate returns my smile. "She's a nice girl," he says. "And I'm not sure that she really wants to seduce your brother. She just doesn't like the fact that he's more interested in your other friend than her." Taken aback by his perception, I run through Avery's attraction to Connor again. I'd assumed it was instantaneous, but now that I think on it—"You're right." I shake my head, marveling that I didn't see it. "I wondered why Avery didn't just take the hint when Connor didn't come running. She's always had her pick of any guy, you know? But now I think on it, the more that Connor's looked at Cass, the more Avery's chased him. You're very perceptive."

Tate grins. "Call it experience. I work on a college campus. My job is just as much relationship counselor as it is history professor, believe me. I spend more time handing out tissues than I do marking papers."

Once again, despite my misgivings I can't help but find myself warming to Tate. He has a gentle way of making everyone feel comfortable. Even Jeremiah's reserve thaws in the face of his charm. Noya arrives, and we all wander off to look at the grounds. We are walking in the direction of the tunnel entrances.

"Antoine is coming back," I say to Noya in a low tone. "I think he wants to talk with you about what you've found here." I don't think it's politic to mention that Jeremiah doesn't trust Tate.

"I wish I had something to tell him." Noya frowns at where Tate and Jeremiah have paused at the freshly poured concrete slab that covers the entrance we broke through only weeks ago. She draws me away to a safe distance under the pretense of pointing at something on the ground. "The concrete over that entrance looks new."

"It is." I choose my words carefully. "We had to break it open recently."

She looks at me sharply. "Why?"

I lower my voice and lead her a little further away. "During the period that the deed was in my maiden name, the cellar was accidentally opened. Antoine and I had to break into the tunnels to get Keziah and Caleb back into the cellar." I swallow, remembering being in the tunnels with Antoine. My blood races at the memory of him drinking from me, holding me so close I could no longer tell where he ended and I began. That memory in turn leads to the one of him holding me against the hard rock, his body pressed against mine as he kissed me. The memory turns my veins to liquid fire, and heat rushes to my face. I turn away from Noya's curious eyes, only to find myself face-to-face with Tate. He is no longer smiling.

"You mentioned your maiden name," he says, no trace of his customary warmth in his voice. "What did you mean by that?"

I look over at the concrete slab where only a moment ago he was standing beside Jeremiah. It's almost fifty yards away. "How did you hear that?" My every nerve ending is tingling on high alert. Noya has taken a step backward and is looking warily at Tate.

Tate grips my shoulders. "Whose name is on the deed to the mansion, Harper?"

"Mine." I force my voice to remain calm. Over by the

concrete, Jeremiah is poking at the entrance, oblivious to the drama unfolding behind him.

Tate's grip tightens, his eyes dark and intent. There's no mistake now. He's trying to compel me. "And what is your surname now, Harper?"

I'm still trying to think of how to reply when another voice, deep and cold enough to freeze the river below, interrupts us.

"Her name is Marigny. And unless you want me to end your existence, I suggest you take your hands off her."

My heart comes to a sharp stop and then starts beating again, so fast and hard it's painful.

Antoine has come home.

CHAPTER 7

BROTHERS

I can feel Antoine as if it were his hands on my shoulders instead of Tate's. He's behind me, only inches from where I stand, yet distant as another country. I can barely breathe. Tate releases me, staring over my shoulder. Any lingering doubts about what Tate is are gone. His surprise at Antoine's presence has stripped the pretense of mortality from his face, leaving the preternatural lines, clear and impossibly still. But even in the sculpted perfection there remains a hint of gentleness, a kind of worn desolation that I can't help but find touching, despite all that has just taken place. I step aside, out of their path, but avoid directly meeting Antoine's eyes. I'm not sure what I'm more afraid of— what I'll see in them, or what he might read in mine.

"Why are you here?" Antoine's voice is as cold and hard as the glare he directs at Tate.

"I heard you were making mistakes," Tate says calmly. "I came to make sure they don't get out of hand."

"Tate." Noya is looking between the two men, frowning. "I didn't realize you knew Antoine."

"Tate? That's the name you're using these days?" Antoine

folds his arms and raises a sardonic eyebrow. The gestures are so achingly familiar they make my heart catch. But Antoine is not looking at me; in fact, I may as well not exist. He has not so much as glanced in my direction.

"Why?" Noya turns to Tate, looking confused. "What is your real name, nephew?"

"Takatoka isn't your nephew." Antoine's tone is dry. "He's your ancestor. I imagine he contrived to cross your path during your journey here and then compelled you to believe he was your relative. He is particularly gifted at diplomacy."

"While Antoine's gift lies in self-preservation," counters Tate. The two eye each other with palpable tension.

"Takatoka." Noya is eyeing Tate with barely disguised awe. "You're a descendant of the Tattooed Serpent?"

"Oh, Takatoka isn't just a descendant. He's the Serpent's designated heir." Antoine's mouth twists at the wonder in Noya's face. "Before he became what I, too, am, Tate, as you call him, was quite the diplomat." He shrugs. "Not quite so much the great warrior required to rise to the power of the Tattooed Serpent, however."

"No." Tate's mouth tightens. "Violence was always more Antoine's speciality. Wasn't it, brother?" Seeing Antoine's face darken, I guess the barb hit home.

"Then you are the one we sing of," says Noya, staring at Antoine. "The man our own people made monster using Natchez magic." Noya is clearly fascinated, though both Antoine and Tate seem largely oblivious to her interest.

"Wait." It is Jeremiah who speaks. He has come up behind me and is looking between the two men, who are still faced off in open hostility. "You two are brothers?"

"Ah." Now it is Tate who folds his arms. "See, we would have been brothers. Should have been. In fact, for a long time, I was under the mistaken belief that we were. But no, Jeremiah, to answer your question—we are not brothers. Not then." He takes a step closer and stares at Antoine, then lets his eyes move very deliberately to rest on me. "And most certainly, not now."

I've stayed silent until this point. Partly because I don't want to interfere in whatever shooting contest is unfolding, and partly because Antoine's proximity seems to cripple my ability to speak. But Tate's remark breaks through my stupor. "Would one of you like to explain what's going on?" I ask, secretly impressed that my voice is so steady.

Tate's eyes drop pointedly to my ring finger. "Yes, Antoine," he says acidly. "Why don't you explain just exactly what is going on?"

Antoine's eyes glitter dangerously. "Whatever you're thinking, you're wrong."

"Oh, I don't think so." Reaching out to grasp my hand, Tate raises it so the late afternoon sun makes the emerald glow. "What is the Marigny emerald doing on her finger, Antoine? It seems to me that nothing has changed—*brother*. Nothing at all. Keziah and Caleb are still in that cellar. And there are still no depths you will not sink to in order to keep them there."

Antoine moves so quickly he is no more than a shadow, knocking Tate's hand from mine. They wheel to face one another, the threat of violence dancing between them like the first lick of lightning on the air before a storm. Their mutual anger upsets me on some deep inner level that causes me to react before I properly think it through.

"Enough." I step between them, facing Antoine. "This isn't helping anything." It occurs to me as I speak that stepping between two angry vampires is possibly not the smartest decision I've made, but somehow that consideration gets lost in the way I feel being this close to Antoine again. Unfortunately, it seems I'm the only one of the two of us affected by it.

"Harper." Antoine doesn't meet my eyes but rather looks just past me, as if I simply don't exist. "Get out of the way."

I try to ignore how much that hurts and turn instead to

focus on Tate. Despite his obvious hostility, I can't help but feel the same subconscious calm I always feel in his presence. There is something almost pained in his expression that makes me even more certain he is not a threat. "Since you clearly know the history," I say to Tate, "you know that we don't have time to argue amongst ourselves. Jeremiah's parents sold my brother and I the Marigny mansion. My brother put my name on the deed." Unlike Antoine, Tate's eyes swivel to me, and I can tell he is listening closely. "In changing the name on the deed, they broke the binding holding Keziah and Caleb in the cellar, meaning Keziah's mind control became stronger. After she began trying to convince me to release her, I forced Antoine to tell me the truth of what's in the cellar. When Antoine told me that the only way to make the binding whole again was to have a Marigny name on the deed, I asked him to marry me to solve the problem."

Despite my efforts to recite the story dispassionately, color floods my face. Even saying the word *marry* takes me back to the small stone church, the scent of magnolias on a summer breeze—and the happiest I have ever felt. I cast a surreptitious glance at Antoine, but he is staring stonily into the distance, apparently entirely unmoved by the recollection of our wedding day. "Keziah and Caleb still managed to escape for a short time. But we got them back into the cellar and sealed it. Then Antoine went in search of someone who could help us break the binding completely."

"Oh, I'm sure he did." Tate seems unimpressed by my story. His eyes harden as they turn back to Antoine. "Just as I'm sure he convinced you it was your idea to marry." His mouth twists in disgust. "Have your years alone so badly corrupted you that your rage has turned to sadism? Could you not have simply compelled the girl to sell you the mansion? Was it really necessary to make her marry you?"

"You're slipping, brother." Now it is Antoine's turn to smile grimly. "Have you not noticed that Harper cannot be compelled?"

Tate glances at me, clearly taken aback. "I thought she must be using frankincense as a shield." Antoine doesn't answer, just raises his eyebrows. Tate frowns. "But that's impossible," he breathes, looking more closely at me.

Antoine tilts his head and folds his arms. I'd forgotten just how infuriating that gesture could be. "You know," I say testily, "I'm right here. And I'm not a subject in a lab experiment. The two of you don't have to talk about me as if I don't exist."

"Wait." Tate is looking between Antoine and I. "If he didn't compel you—do you mean that marrying him was your idea?" He looks at me curiously. "Even after you knew what he was?"

The blood roars under my skin, turning it blazing red beneath the flyaway curls touching my face. I force myself to meet Tate's eyes. "It was my idea," I say quietly. Tate's eyes swivel to Antoine.

"And you agreed to this." There's an odd note in his voice, as if he is as curious as he is critical.

When Antoine doesn't immediately answer, I cut my eyes sideways, in time to see his fists clench then abruptly release. I'm not the only one who catches the gesture. Tate's eyebrows shoot up, then a slow smile curves the edges of his mouth. "Well, brother," he murmurs. "Perhaps some things do change, after all."

I want to know what he means by that, what might have changed in Antoine. What he was like before. In fact, I'd like to take Tate away, lock him in a room, and compel him to tell me everything about Antoine that he knows.

Antoine, however, seems as unlikely to share his thoughts as he's ever been. He's staring down the slope, to where the fairy lights are beginning to glow in the growing dusk. "Are you planning some kind of party?" he asks abruptly.

"It's Avery's birthday. She wanted to have it here." I can hear the slightly defensive tone to my voice. I have a feeling I know exactly what Antoine will think of that idea.

He doesn't disappoint.

Antoine swings around to face me and, for the first time since his unexpected arrival, he actually meets my eyes. "Are you completely insane?" he demands. He's so close I can see the gold flecks in his eyes, smell the faint, spicy scent of cedar that makes my senses reel. His shirt is open at the neck and all I can think of is touching the tanned skin beneath it. I swallow hard.

"It's our home," I say instead. "We can't hide forever."

"I leave you alone for a matter of weeks, and this is what you do?" His voice is rough. "Do you have a death wish, Harper?"

"Marrying you would suggest she might," comes Tate's dry rejoinder behind us. "And leaving has always been your specialty—*brother*." This time, there is no mistaking the heavy irony in his tone.

I wonder if the hostility between them upsets me so much because I no longer have my own sister to bicker with, to share history with. Whatever the nature of the relationship between Antoine and Tate, it is clearly very old and runs as deeply as any familial bond. I find myself oddly impatient with them both.

"That's enough now." I fold my own arms and look at Tate. "I've told you my story. Now it's time for yours. You might want to start with the woman in the sketch you showed me. Who is she?"

Tate opens his mouth to answer, but Antoine cuts over him.

"The woman in the sketch was my sister." His voice is cold and clinical, and he doesn't look at me when he speaks. "Her name was Marguerite Marigny. She and Takatoka were in love with one another."

Tate makes a soft noise and steps backward, turning his face slightly away so I can't read his eyes.

"They planned to marry," Antoine continues in the same hard voice. "Even though it meant defying my father and incurring public disgrace. On my sister's part, at least." Tate's face tightens visibly, but he doesn't interrupt. Antoine's face, by comparison, is dark and unreadable. "But those plans were all before Keziah and Caleb came to the plantation. After that, everything changed. My sister was the only living Marigny left untouched by their madness. There was nobody else but Marguerite to inherit the mansion and hold the binding after I was turned, and Keziah and Caleb were caught."

I'm not the only one mesmerized by the story. Jeremiah and Noya are looking between the two in open fascination. I know exactly how they feel, as if they've stepped through the looking glass, or into the wardrobe that leads to Narnia. Hearing two people discuss events that took place almost three centuries earlier as if they had happened yesterday is strangely dislocating.

"What your husband isn't saying," says Tate, placing a sardonic emphasis on the word *husband*, "is that he believed that if Marguerite married me, society would not permit her to inherit. He was convinced she would have been cast out in disgrace. Hanged, even, so fierce was French hatred toward the Nachez. They thought us no better than animals, even worse than the slaves they kept, who at least had monetary value. But neither, Antoine believed, could Marguerite inherit the mansion if she remained unmarried. And besides," he continues, the bitterness in his tone unmistakeable, "without a husband, she couldn't produce an heir to inherit the Marigny binding. And by then, the binding was all that mattered, Antoine, was it not?"

Tate's eyes are dark with old anger and pain. He doesn't wait for Antoine to respond, doesn't even look at him, before he goes on. "In order to ensure that she remained in the mansion, and in possession of her inheritance, Antoine told Marguerite she had to make a marriage society would accept. But Marguerite refused to marry anyone else. She loved me, and she was determined to have me, even if it meant facing the scorn of all those she knew. I was equally determined to marry her."

I'm looking between them, still not understanding. Antoine has turned his back to us. Tate is staring at his stiff-backed figure as if he wants to say something else but doesn't know how. In the end, it is Noya who speaks.

"He turned you," she says, looking between Tate and Antoine. "Antoine made you a vampire so that you couldn't marry his sister."

I feel my heart stop, then start beating again. When Antoine turns around, he faces me directly, ignoring everyone else present. I feel a faint shock as his eyes meet mine. His face is as still and cold as marble, but his eyes blaze with an emotion I cannot read. "Yes," he says simply. "I made Tate a vampire." He holds my eyes for a long moment, as if he's searching for an answer in them. I want to speak, but I can find no reason among the thousand half-formed questions swirling in my mind. I watch the blazing light in his eyes fade, feel him draw away from me, as powerless to stop it as I am to make sense of what I've just heard.

"Now that we all understand the family history," he says in a flat, hard tone, turning away again, "can we discuss how we are going to stop this ridiculous party from taking place?"

CHAPTER 8

CRUELTY

*A*n awkward silence is broken by Avery, Cass, and Connor all arriving at the same time, spilling from their cars in a sea of chatter which, under the circumstances, is not unwelcome.

"Harper!" cries Avery, hurtling toward me. "I ran into some friends from across the river and invited them to my party. I figured you'd be fine"—she catches sight of Antoine and comes to an abrupt halt, her eyes narrowing. "The sexy uncle," she says, in a not-altogether-friendly tone, looking between Antoine and me. "You're back."

Connor, not far behind her, seems scarcely less pleased. "Antoine." His eyes go slightly unfocused for a moment. "I thought I wouldn't see you again."

I remember Antoine compelling him on the night we sealed the cellar: *After tonight you won't ever have to see me again.*

"Well, he's back." Jeremiah's voice is so unabashedly happy that Connor looks at Antoine with a slightly less hostile expression. From the corner of my eye, I notice Tate watching the exchanges with a faintly bemused expression.

"Tate." I turn to him, eager to escape the growing complexity of the dynamic. "Didn't you want to see the rest of the mansion? I'll show you around." I also intend to shamelessly pump Tate for any and all information about the story I've just heard. Antoine clearly knows me well enough to know that, because his face clouds over like a tropical storm.

Ignoring Antoine's glowering eyes on my back, I walk toward the mansion, Tate close behind. "He won't back down on this party, you understand," says Tate as we move out of earshot. "And I'm not sure he's wrong. Having a party here is not a very wise decision, under the current circumstances."

"Nor is having two vampires in my home, but here we are." I'm unable to keep the edge from my tone. Tate casts me a sideways look as we go up the front steps. "So you were trying to compel me, earlier." It's dark inside the mansion. I flick the hanging switch that turns on lights Connor has strung up to act as a substitute until he gets all the wiring redone. They cast a mellow glow across the peeling plaster and chipped tile. I think, as I often do, that I will almost be sad when we have proper lighting. Somehow the hanging lights seem to suit the old mansion, giving it a comforting, warm feel.

"Yes, I confess I was trying to compel you." Tate's smile is as warm and open as ever, despite the shadow of recent emotion behind his eyes. "I thought you must be wearing or taking frankincense."

"How does that work, the frankincense thing?"

He shrugs. "You can burn it as incense, or wear it, or take it in raw form. It's one of the reasons for the legends about crosses and vampires. It isn't crucifixes that are harmful, or holy water. It's the frankincense burned inside the churches in which those things tend to be found. Even the faintest inhalation of frankincense will cripple our kind, almost instantly." He smiles wryly as I take out a pitcher for tea and put the kettle on. "The New Age movement has been hell for vampires. Do you have any idea how many hippy shops burn frankincense outside the door? They say it raises their vibration, whatever that means."

I can't help but laugh at that. I think again that it really is difficult not to like Tate. He has the same wry humor, and understated strength, as Antoine. I feel a surge of sadness that there seems to be such a rift between them.

"Frankincense can be worked into jewelry," Tate goes on. "Some people even chew it. Though it is never certain how long it will stay in the system, I can certainly attest to how toxic it is to a vampire—the taste of frankincense taints the blood, making it undrinkable. I have seen people put raw frankincense in their water bottles, and that seems to work just as effectively, at least as long as the water stays in their system." He looks at me curiously. "It seems, though, that for some reason you don't need it."

I don't answer that. I'm not sure why I can't be compelled. At this stage, it's just one more mystery to add to a life already overflowing with them, and it seems by far the least pressing issue we face. I pour water into a large pot of tea that I set aside to steep. Taking a stool from the corner, I put it against the wall so I can reach the herbs growing in the window box.

"Why did you come here?" I'm leaning through the window, so he can't see my face. "You aren't a Marigny. You couldn't have felt the seal open. What made you decide to visit?"

"I might not be a Marigny, but those of my blood created the binding. I'm forever tied to this earth. I feel everything connected to it." His voice hardens. "Especially when it comes to that binding."

I turn from snipping peppermint and look at him. "I'm sorry about Marguerite," I say quietly, meaning it. "I can't begin to imagine how hard it must have been for you both."

"Of course you can imagine." The edge in his voice makes me put the scissors down and give him my full attention. "A human in love with a vampire? After seeing you today, I believe you can imagine that perfectly." I step down off the stool, my face coloring. "But you are right about it being hard for Marguerite." Tate's tone softens slightly, maybe because he can see how uncomfortable I am. "What you can't imagine is the pain of being on the other side. Of watching the person you love marry someone else, make a life with him. Have children with him."

"Did she really do that?"

"I compelled her to do that."

I look at him in surprise. His mouth twists in a pained smile, and behind the kindness in his eyes lingers the shadow of old hurt. "After I woke to my new form, I knew it could never be." Tate shook his head. "I couldn't bear for Marguerite to spend her years longing for something that she could never have. She needed to live her life, just as the binding needed a Marigny heir. I found a good man, a French soldier who I knew would treat her kindly. I compelled her to love him and to forget me. They were married for over twenty years."

"What about you? What did you do?"

"I tried to leave." He looks away for a moment. "I did, for a time. But I always came back. I couldn't bear to stay away from her long. After her husband died, when she was old and alone, I undid the compulsion. I stayed with her then, until the end." He gives me the ghost of a smile. "She's buried not far from here, beneath a tree we planted together. I come back every year on the anniversary of her death."

I stare at him, trying and failing to imagine such a life. "How did she forgive you? For compelling her to marry someone else?" I think of how I would feel if I discovered my whole life had been a lie. "How could she bear it?"

"She was angry at first. But she was married a long time, remember. Long enough to know her husband for the good man he was, and to love him, in her own way. And she adored her children. She was sad, yes. But in the end, she understood why I had to do what I did, and she forgave me for it. Antoine, though, was a different matter. She never forgave him for what he did to me."

"Why did he do that to you?" I whisper. "Why would he be so cruel?"

For a moment shadows chase over Tate's face. "We are all capable of cruelty," he says softly. "Especially when we first turn. He left soon after he turned me. He didn't return for nearly a full lifetime." I consider those words. I had known that Antoine killed his brothers when he first emerged from the cellar as a vampire, mad with thirst. That I could understand. But to brutally condemn an innocent man to his own dark fate—that, I can't understand at all. Perhaps more selfishly, I can't understand why Antoine told me none of this before now. His hard expression when he spoke of it bore no resemblance to the man who married me on a fragrant summer's day or kissed me with blinding heat in an underground tunnel. I don't know who this new Antoine is—and I'm not sure I want to know.

"Is your relationship with Marguerite the reason the Natchez helped Antoine bind Keziah and Caleb?" It's something I've wondered ever since I first heard the story. "I find it hard to imagine why the Natchez would want to help a plantation owner with anything."

"Indirectly. And it wasn't the only reason, but it was one of them." Tate looks at me as if measuring how much to say.

"Antoine hasn't told me much." I turn to chopping mint to hide the color flaming on my face. It hurts to admit how little I know.

"Did he tell you he'd left his family, long before Keziah and Caleb came?"

"Yes." That much I'd known.

"Well, when he left, it was with me." I look up in surprise. Tate gives me a small smile. "We really were as close as brothers. We were that way from when we first met, as children. I taught Antoine to hunt. By the time we were the age you are now, we were inseparable, a friendship neither of our families liked overmuch, though Antoine often said he was more at home among the Natchez than with his own people." He smiles with reminiscence. "When Antoine told me he wanted to leave his family, make a new start with his own trapping business inland, I didn't hesitate to go with him. We were going to be trading partners." His mouth twists slightly. "Of course, I was also in love with his sister, so there was that."

I can't hide my curiosity. "Did Antoine mind?"

"About Marguerite and I? No, not in the beginning. He was happy for us. His father, you know, was a violent, angry man. Antoine had little love for him or his brothers. He planned to make enough money to come back and take his mother and sister away from all of them."

"You said my ring belonged to her." The peppermint lies forgotten on the cutting board, and I've taken a seat at the table. I'm drinking in every word he says, praying Antoine won't interrupt us until I've heard it all. "Where did it come from originally?"

"It belonged to Madeleine, Antoine and Marguerite's mother, whom they both loved, very much." Taking my hand, Tate turns it over in his own, brown eyes lit with reminiscence as he looks at the emerald. "Before Keziah and Caleb came, back when Antoine and I were friends—brothers, even—trapping inland, he gave me the ring. He told me that he feared his mother had already begun to escape his father's cruelty by slipping into madness. Antoine had taken it when he left. He cared nothing, back then, for his family's pride or name. He gave the ring to me so that I could gift it to Marguerite on our wedding. He feared that his mother would lose the ring, or his brothers trade it for coin. Antoine said that he didn't want to see his sister sold into a marriage of his father's choosing. He handed me the ring, and told me I had his blessing. Ironic, really, given what was to come."

Shaking his head, Tate takes a deep breath and shrugs as he gives me a resigned smile. "Anyway. Antoine was our ally in a marriage that we all knew would mean Marguerite's public disgrace." His smile twists. "But then my family sent word that one of our villages had been attacked. It was the first we'd heard of Keziah and Caleb. My friendship with Antoine, and my relationship with his sister, had the unfortunate effect of drawing the fury of Antoine's father and brothers, who were by then quite mad with vampire blood. Antoine and I set off for Deepwater the next day, both worried for Marguerite. We got back to discover that my family had taken Marguerite already. She'd gone with them willingly, trusting them, because of me. But they hadn't taken her to keep her safe."

"They planned to use her blood for their magic." I don't realize I've spoken aloud until Tate's eyes swivel back to me.

"Yes."

I shake my head, lost for words. Tate lifts his shoulders. "Prejudice wasn't the sole preserve of the French. The Natchez had once encouraged marriage outside the tribe, but they disliked the Marigny family, particularly after the arrival of Keziah and Caleb. My family didn't like my relationship with Marguerite any more than hers did.

"I did give the ring to her, eventually. When I compelled her to marry another man. Marguerite never took it off. She wore it until the day before she died, when Antoine came to visit her. By then I'd undone the compulsion, and she knew the truth of what he'd done."

"What did Antoine say to her?" I know I shouldn't ask, but I can't help myself. "When he came to see her?"

"I don't know." Tate meets my eyes, and I can see only sadness and honesty in his. "I wasn't there when he came, and I never knew what he said. All Marguerite told me was that she could never forgive him for what he did to me, to us, and that she'd given him back the ring. She said no daughter of hers would ever wear something so cursed, and that she did not wish to be buried wearing a ring that symbolized all she had been forced to give up. She said she hoped that every time he looked at the ring, Antoine would be forced to remember the pain he had caused her—and the love he had made her lose." Tate's eyes are sad and far away, lost in the past. "Marguerite believed in hope. She thought we could have found a way to stay together and still keep the binding closed. She never forgave Antoine for taking that choice away from us both."

I stare at the emerald on my finger. Since the moment Antoine slid it onto my hand, I have loved it, have felt as if it were a silent witness to our happiness and a promise that perhaps, somehow, there was a way we could be together some-day. Even now that I know the story behind the ring, I cannot help but feel connected to it. But I also can't help but wonder why he chose the emerald, of all things, to give to me. Something so bound to pain and loss—how could it ever be a symbol of hope?

"What about you?" I look at Tate. "What do you believe?"

Tate lifts one shoulder. "I stopped asking myself those questions long ago." He catches my hand again, holding the emerald up to the light as he had earlier. His eyes are full of the empathy that's put me at ease from the beginning, made me instinctively trust him despite all the reasons I have not to. "I have known Antoine Marigny for three centuries, Harper. He is many things, all of them complicated. But I do know this: the fact that he has put that ring on your finger means something. And the fact that he has not run far away from you—has done the opposite, in fact, and not only married you, but returned here—means something even more. I gave up, long ago, ever expecting Antoine to change or to surprise me. But in marrying you, it seems he might have done both." Letting go of my hand, he steps back. "I can only hope," he says, to himself more than me, "that the change is for good, and that he means no harm here."

"How is it that you don't hate him?" I search his face. "That you can forgive him—after everything he did to you?"

Tate stares past me, but I know it isn't the driveway he's looking down, but a longer road, to the past he and Antoine share.

"If you had known the man he was before all of this," he says slowly, "you would know why I cannot hate him. And if you understood how he became what he is, you would feel nothing but pity." The centuries he has lived seem to glow behind his youthful exterior, like the mellow sheen on old, polished wood. "But do not think either of us a victim, Harper. Neither Antoine nor I are blameless. If you might take one piece of wisdom from all the years I have lived, then let it be this." He smiles at me sadly. "Nothing is ever as simple as it seems."

CHAPTER 9

LIES

I leave the tea and peppermint with Tate in the kitchen, planning to head out back to the garden. I've never felt such a need to thrust my hands into dirt, lose myself in the mundane tasks of digging, weeding, planting. Tate's story has left me with so much to sift through that I barely know where to start, let alone how I feel, or what any of it might mean for my own future. I've barely got to the corridor when Cass appears.

"Harper." She catches my arm. "I don't know what to do about Avery."

I feel an uncharacteristic urge to snap at her that I couldn't care less about Avery. Cass looks at me more closely and frowns. "Are you okay, Harper? You look like you've seen a ghost."

My laugh sounds jarring to my ears. I take my arm out of her grasp and try to calm my voice. Antoine's arrival and Tate's story have left me scattered. It's a huge effort just to focus on what Cass is saying.

"Avery?" I force myself to look interested. "Why are you

worried about her?" The sound of chatter floats through the back door. "They all sound happy enough out there."

"She's acting weird." Cass frowns. "All she could talk about all day at school was coming out here to decorate for the party. But Jeremiah told me that the moment she got here, she left again, in Tate's car, no less. And my mom called just now. Apparently, when she left here, Avery went to Witch Way. Mom mentioned it because she thought Avery seemed a little off."

"Your mom's shop? What would she want to buy there?"

"That's just it. I don't know. I can't imagine there's anything in there that would help with her party. Avery's off-balance, some-how. One moment she's all over Connor, to the point where it's embarrassing. The next she can't get enough of Tate. Now it sounds like she's invited all kinds of randoms to the party, and that just isn't like Avery. She's normally such a control freak." Cass shakes her head. "There's something going on with her. And now that Antoine is back, Jeremiah will probably be spending more time with him, and..." her voice trails off, and she looks at me uncertainly.

"You're worried that she'll feel even more left out," I guess. Cass nods.

"Well, I wouldn't worry about that." I glance out the back door to where Antoine is glaring up toward the mansion. His eyes sear my skin. "Antoine probably won't stay long. He's barely speaking to me. He isn't at all happy about this party."

"Why would he be talking to you? And why would he concern himself with your party?" Cass looks at me curiously. "Actually, why is Antoine here at all? Were you two actually dating, Harper?" I mentally curse, remembering that Cass has no idea Antoine has ever been anything more to me than Jere-miah's uncle. I'm saved from more questions to which I don't have answers by Avery bounding through the door. She comes to an abrupt halt when she sees us talking.

"What are you talking about?" Her voice is oddly high-pitched and breathless, her eyes glittering strangely. "Is it about me?"

"We're just a little worried about you," Cass says, putting her hand out. "Avery—are you okay?"

"I'm fine." She tosses her head, but in the moment before she turns away, I realize the glittering in her eyes is from tears rather than anger, and I feel real concern. "You can talk to us," I say gently, touching her shoulder. She feels hot through her blouse and her shoulder is hard with tension.

Cass steps forward. "If it's about Connor," she begins in a soft voice. Avery swings around, her face red, and Cass takes a wary step back.

"I know all about you and Connor." Avery's voice is brittle with hurt. "I'm not blind, Cass. I know it was you, not me, that he came to pick up from school today. I've seen the way he looks at you."

"Avery, I didn't mean to hurt you." Cass throws me a worried look, but Avery is already turning away dismissively.

"It doesn't matter." I can hear the hurt and loneliness in her voice. "I don't care about him, anyway." I reach out to her, but Avery dodges the gesture and moves toward the hallway. "Honestly," she says, in a falsely bright voice, not looking at us. "I'm happy for you both, Cass. I just want to focus on the party and having a good time. And if you two really *are* my friends"—she gives us both a challenging stare over her shoulder—"you'll stop talking about me and instead help me make it the best party of the year."

"Of course, Avery—" we begin to reassure her, but she's already gone.

Cass turns to me. "That was weird."

I nod. Avery can be vain and inconsiderate, but I've never considered her unstable before.

"I didn't think she cared that much about Connor. I thought

he was just another conquest." Cass looks worried. "Maybe I should back off—"

"No." I take her by the arm. "Whatever has got to Avery, it shouldn't affect you and Connor. You're the best thing to happen to him in a long time, believe me."

"Really?" The expression on her face is so hopeful, and yet so doubting, that I can't help but hug her.

"Really." I smile into her shoulder. Amid all the crazy that has just been unleashed in my life, it's almost comforting to be immersed in teen drama for a moment. And I am genuinely happy for Cass and Connor. I know they'll be good for each other, and if anyone deserves some happiness, it's my brother. My thoughts start to wander dangerously toward Tate's story and Antoine, and I'm almost glad when I hear Connor's boots on the floorboards. I release Cass as he appears in the doorway from the side corridor.

"Hey." He gives Cass a crooked smile and then looks at me. "What's wrong with Avery? I just found her coming out of the library—again. That's the third time. And I've already put up the barrier tape to keep people out. She shouldn't be going in there."

"She's just upset about something." I try not to react to the news that Avery, or anyone else for that matter, has been anywhere near the library. "I think she probably wanted to have a cry in peace. I'll go and find her."

"Well, tell her to cry somewhere else," says Connor, unmoved. "That room isn't safe."

That's the understatement of the century.

I nod, hoping I, at least, appear normal, and leave him with Cass, heading out through the back door. If I'm honest, after my conversation with Tate, I just need a moment to take a beat.

When Tate talks about Antoine, I feel as if he's describing a stranger. Every word he said served to remind me just how little I know about the man I married, where he's come from, what he went through all those years ago.

I think back to when I asked Antoine to marry me. "Even if we were of the same time," he'd said, "I would still be six years older than you."

That age gap had seemed laughable to me at the time. What's six years, after all, in comparison to three centuries?

But after hearing Tate's story, those years have a different shape in my mind. By the time Antoine was turned into a vampire, he had lived a whole life. Become a man independent enough to walk away from his inheritance, start a business elsewhere. In wild, unknown country, going by what Tate said. For some odd reason, that lone fact impresses upon me in a way nothing else has until this point just how much life separates Antoine and I. *He was walking this earth when America was young.*

I feel as if all that should be enough to make me pause, to regret my decision. As I have many times since the day I stood in that church, I wonder at the strange certainty in my heart that guided me that day and has ever since. I wonder why it is that the years Antoine has lived, the life he had before he was turned, don't alter my inner conviction that we are somehow inherently right for one another. And then I remember the cold, hard look in his eye when we met earlier and wonder why I'm concerning myself with how right he is or isn't for me, when it seems that Antoine himself couldn't care less.

Standing on the back porch, I can't see Antoine among the group by the dock tending to Avery's party decorations. My stomach clenches. *What if he's left already?* I think, with a sudden lurch of dread. *What if he isn't going to even talk to me?*

"This party is a bad idea." I swing around, my every nerve tingling. Antoine is leaning against the wall, deep in the twilight shadows. He's staring out at the fairy lights by the dock. "You know it's dangerous for people to be in this house."

"Of course I know that." I'm proud that my voice sounds almost normal. My skin is prickling, and whatever it is that I'm feeling, it certainly isn't normal.

"Then why did you agree to host a party?" His face is shadowed, and I can't read the expression in his eyes.

"I'm not sure." I speak slowly, unsure of what I'm going to say until the words come out. "I guess I just felt—" I break off and turn away, realizing that what I was about to say was the wrong thing.

"You felt what, Harper?" He's moved away from the wall. I can feel him, right behind me, his presence so strong and rich it's like feeling a river at my back, one that threatens at any moment to pull me into a current I cannot fight. "What feeling was so strong it convinced you that having a party above that cellar would be a good idea?"

His voice is resigned rather than angry. After so long keeping my secrets, of being perpetually on guard, his nearness threatens my composure in a way even Tate's story didn't.

"Lonely," I whisper. "I felt lonely."

I forgot how he has this effect on me, of drawing forth the emotions I can't show others. In the silence that follows, I'm terribly aware of him standing so close, and I feel foolish for showing him my vulnerability. In all the visions I had of Antoine's return, there was no version in which I sounded pathetic and lost, and the long pause that follows my admission isn't reassuring.

When he does finally speak, his voice is low. "It's better if I'm not here."

"Better for whom?" I turn around to find him standing only inches away, close enough to touch. I clench my fists to ensure I don't. I'm afraid of how much I want to. "Not for Jeremiah," I say. "He misses you. He's got no family here, nobody who understands what he's been through."

"He'll make friends."

"It isn't friends he needs. He needs family."

"Having family isn't a cure for loneliness."

"Then what is?" My voice isn't entirely steady. I take a deep breath and force myself to look at him. "You didn't give either of us a choice. You just left."

One of his hands comes up toward me, then falls away. "If I'd thought staying would help either of you," he says roughly, "I would have stayed, Harper."

His nearness unsettles me. I move backwards, out of reach. I don't trust myself if he touches me. I don't know what I feel, or how to ask what I want to know. There's so much between us that is dark and confusing, and I'm wary of how easy it is for me to lose control over my feelings when we talk. I find myself intentionally thinking about things that don't involve feelings at all, and so I ask something that's been niggling at me since seeing him and Tate together. "What did you and Noya mean when you called Tate the Tattooed Serpent?"

Antoine makes an impatient noise. "It doesn't matter anymore. All of that was a long time ago, Harper."

"It matters to me." I fold my arms and stare at him from a safe distance. He sighs. His mouth twitches in a rueful smile.

"I forgot how stubborn you can be," he murmurs.

"And I forgot how annoying *you* can be." I try to ignore the way my heart jumps at his smile. *This is the man who turned his friend into a vampire,* I remind myself. *The man who deprived his sister of a lifetime of happiness.*

Somehow, knowing that doesn't change how I feel when he looks at me.

"Fine." His tone is now more amused than cold. "I told you before that the Natchez were ruled by a leader called the Great Sun."

"It was the Great Sun whose name is on the treaty."

Antoine nods. "The Great Sun ruled the Natchez, but in the tribal structure, the Tattooed Serpent was just as important. He was both war chief and diplomat. In my time, it was the Tattooed Serpent who negotiated the treaty and led the Natchez against Keziah and Caleb. Takatoka—Tate—was a son of the

Great Sun, and the appointed successor of the Tattooed Serpent. He was raised to lead the warriors of his tribe and to be skilled at negotiation." He pauses. "He was also my best friend. And in love with my sister."

Night has fallen with the suddenness of the South, the evening birdsong so loud it covers the sound of his voice. When I move closer to hear him, his nearness fills the air about me, as intoxicating as the crushed moonflowers on the ground about us. "When the Natchez took my sister, planning to use her to wield their magic, Tate begged me to help, to stand in her place. I didn't need him to beg. I was as horrified as he was at the thought of my sister being hurt. There was never a thought of saying no, not when I realized they would use Marguerite if I refused. And especially not after Tate's mother explained that she would have to die in order to create the magic that would hold them. It was an unimaginable sacrifice, an incredibly self-less act. Atsila had no reason to love my family. But she'd looked into the fire and seen something that convinced her it was the only way." An odd expression crosses his face. "I've never truly understood what she saw."

"Atsila was Tate's mother?" No wonder, I think, that Tate was so shocked when I said it earlier.

"She was. Her death was a great loss to the Natchez, to Tate especially."

No wonder Tate harbours so much anger. I brace myself to ask the question I've been dancing around, the one question in the whole story that I simply don't understand.

"Why did you do what you did to Tate?" I ask, searching his face. "You made the choice to sacrifice yourself to bind Keziah and Caleb. Tate's own mother died to make it happen. Why, then, would you ruin Tate's life—and your sister's happiness— by turning him? Wasn't there some other way to ensure the binding remained in place?"

Antoine's face has closed over as I speak, and now he steps

away from me, the distance between us feeling empty and cold. Whatever intimacy we tentatively re-established is gone as fleetingly as it came, replaced by the hard mask I remember all too well.

"Ah." He is the mocking stranger once more. "Tate hasn't held back from relaying the darkest details of the family history, I take it."

"I would rather hear you tell it." I reach out to touch his face, but he pulls away before I can.

"I told you once before." Antoine is in the shadows again, his face hard to read. "The terrible stories might not have been true at the beginning—but they have all been true in the years since." The words rap onto my mind like falling stones, and I remember when he last spoke them, in the darkness of the tunnels, just before he kissed me. "Don't look for any good reasons for the actions I took then. You won't find any. Don't try to look for redemption for me, Harper. The time is long past when you might find it."

"I don't believe that," I whisper.

"You should." He steps into the light, and I can once again see his face clearly. It is hard and remote, and he holds himself away from me, as distant and unreachable as a foreign shore. "Whatever the worst is that you are thinking, you would still not be close to imagining me as I was then. I was every bit the monster of legend. And make no mistake—for all his amiable exterior, Tate is just as capable of horror as I am. We are vampires, Harper." He says it with cold finality. "Don't seek to make us men." He jumps off the porch and sinks silently to the earth. In an instant he is gone from view, leaving me staring at the lights by the river and listening to the laughter of my friends.

CHAPTER 10

PRESENTS

I barely sleep at all.

Jeremiah left with barely a backward glance earlier, unable to hide his excitement at Antoine's return. Despite my own inner unrest, I can't help but feel glad that he has family close by again, even if only for a short time. I know Antoine won't stay. I'm not certain I want him to.

I toss and turn beneath the fairy lights on my bed frame, turning Tate's and Antoine's words over in my mind, comparing them, searching for similarities and discrepancies. Although the stories they told sound superficially the same, to my mind, there are some glaring differences.

Tate said of Antoine that if I "understood how he became what he is," that I would not judge him so harshly. Antoine, though, cut himself no such slack. He seemed, if anything, to believe that I didn't know the worst of what he was.

I remember back to when Antoine first told me the truth about being a vampire. Back then, I'd been all too ready to believe the worst, even accusing him of murdering Jeremiah's family. He'd done nothing to correct my perception, even after I'd learned the truth, insisting instead that I should be under no illusions as to what he was then or is now. Exactly as he said again tonight.

Part of me knows that regardless of the details, the essence of what Antoine says is true. Even through the fog of emotion that clouds my judgment whenever he gets close to me, I can sense the violent undercurrent in him. I don't for a moment doubt that he's a killer, and that he's been a ruthless one. I can feel the savagery inside him, a dark thrill that is both potent and disturbing. The question is whether or not the savagery is the essence of what he is—or simply a part of him. Perhaps those distinctions shouldn't matter. But the reality is that I know that darkness myself, know that it lives in us all.

I remember one night sitting by Tessa's bed. It had been in the final weeks of her life. The time for false hopes had long passed, and we all knew we were simply marking the days, no matter what we said aloud. Tessa was sleeping, and the hospital was quiet. I'd looked down at her pale, gaunt face, and felt a rush of anger so deep and visceral it physically hurt. I almost hated her in that moment. For leaving me, for the haunted look I saw in Connor's eyes whenever I looked at him, for the life I would be left with, a twin without my other half. In that long, excruciating moment, I truly wanted my own sister dead. It was only when I discovered I was clutching a pillow so hard my knuckles were white that I realized, in horror, that I'd been almost moments away from putting it over Tessa's face.

I'd left the hospital and sat down by a fountain in the mall and cried, so much a concerned old man sweeping the pavement came over to ask if I was okay. I wasn't. I'd touched a darkness inside myself I hadn't known existed until that moment.

So, yes, I have a little knowledge of darkness. And what would such darkness be, I wonder, if it was accelerated by vampire blood, by the urge to kill? How difficult would it be to put the pillow down, so to speak, then?

I know it's not the same thing. But it's all I have to under-stand the man Antoine is. And I want to understand him. I want to understand all of this.

My restless mind gets me out of bed over and over, and by the time morning comes, I'm jittery and unsettled with lack of sleep.

It's the day of Avery's party.

I'm drinking coffee in the dawn stillness when I see Noya's rental pull into the driveway, hers the only figure behind the wheel.

"Hey." Her sunglasses are pushed up onto her head, and in the early morning light her eyes are red and tired. It looks like I'm not the only one who had a sleepless night. "I came to say goodbye." She mounts the steps and sits beside me. I guess my disappointment shows, because she gives me a small smile, her lips pressed together. "I'm sorry. But I'm in the middle of some-thing here that is way past my skills. I need to consult people who understand more about what you're dealing with. I'm afraid that if I intervene, I'll only make things worse."

I return her smile. "I know how you feel."

She laughs softly. "I'm going to give you my number, Harper. Call me anytime. Even if it's just to talk."

"Talk about what?" I say, without thinking.

She raises her eyebrows at me then looks down at the ring on my hand. "I'd say there's more than one thing on your mind."

I nod ruefully. "Thanks." She puts her number into my phone and I notice again how beat she looks. "You know, you should probably get some sleep before you drive. You look exhausted."

"Yeah, well." A cloud passes over her face. "Exhausted seems like a permanent state for me, lately." She stands up without waiting for an answer, and I get the feeling there's a lot more to her words than just a sleepless night. "Maybe I will see you again,

Harper." She puts out her hand and I shake it, but something tells me that Noya isn't coming back. I don't blame her. I guess vampires and curses are a fun hobby—until they're actually real.

Cass arrives at midday. By the lingering kiss she and Connor exchange on the front lawn when they think I'm not watching, it's clear their relationship has moved on from the flirting stage. I smile to myself and stay out of sight, though I can't help but worry a little about Avery's reaction, particularly on the day of her party. For a fleeting moment I consider asking Tate for help. His good looks and endless charm would distract Avery, and for some reason I can't quite understand, I trust him. I'm playing the whole thing out in my head before it occurs to me that a three-century-old vampire with a broken heart that doesn't seem to have healed isn't really ideal boyfriend material. That in turn makes me look at the emerald on my finger, and by the time Cass comes into the kitchen, I'm well and truly ready to be distracted.

"Avery was at Mom's shop again this morning." Cass puts a box of lurid-colored alcoholic drinks on the table. I cast them a wary glance and make a mental note to stick to Connor's terrible punch.

"She's been going there a lot," I remark, unpacking the snacks she's brought.

"I know." Cass frowns. "So far this week she's bought tarot cards, a book on astrology, and at least three ugly rings I'm sure she'll never wear, just like I'm sure she hasn't opened either the cards or the book."

"Then why?"

"Oh, come on." Connor comes into the kitchen and slips his arms around Cass's waist from behind. She casts me a worried glance, then relaxes when I smile. "Avery's hoping Tate will be there." Connor reaches around Cass and grabs a handful of the pretzels she's pouring into a bowl, grinning as she slaps his hand away. "I should know her tactics," he goes on. "She's been lying in wait for me for months."

"Ego, much?" Cass says, but she's smiling. "I hope it works out for her with Tate," she goes on, her brow furrowing. "Avery deserves someone nice." Connor makes a dismissive noise. I glare at him and he subsides. Since I can't exactly share Cass's hopes for Avery's romantic future with Tate, I keep my thoughts to myself.

"Is Jeremiah's uncle coming tonight?" Connor's tone is deceptively casual, but I'm not fooled.

"No idea." I suspect Connor is as unconvinced by my tone as I am by his. I turn away and busy myself with decorations.

When Avery does arrive mid-afternoon, Jeremiah is driving her car. She climbs out unsteadily, waving a bottle of champagne at me. "Oh, Lord," I mutter to Cass. "You get the bottle. I'll try to sober her up." I shoot Jeremiah an accusatory look and he opens his hands in a helpless gesture. "She was already like this when I found her," he says defensively as I get close. "At least I got her to give me the keys."

"Harper!" Avery shrieks, throwing her arms around my neck and breathing champagne fumes all over me. "It's my birthday!"

"I know." I smile as I disentangle myself. "And it's my job to make sure you're the most stunning girl here. Come upstairs so I can give you your present."

"Ooh! Presents!" Momentarily distracted, Avery gives Connor no more than a cursory glance as she passes him, thrusting the half empty, warm bottle of champagne at Cass as she goes. "You can have that," she says haughtily, before taking a very unsteady path up the wide staircase. Rolling my eyes at Cass, I steer Avery into my room and hand her a large, flat package wrapped in gift paper. She tears eagerly at the wrapping until the painting beneath is revealed. "Oh, Harper," she breathes, all trace of tipsy drama queen gone. "It's beautiful." She stares at the painting. "I can't believe that's me."

I've painted her as I saw her the day we were on the dock, when she asked if she could have her party at the mansion. She's staring out over the river, the late afternoon sun catching the bronze in her eyes and the sheen of her hair. I tried to catch the strength and loneliness I feel inside her, the depths I know are there, that she struggles so hard to hide. She looks at me now and, to my surprise, I see her mouth tremble and unshed tears glisten in her eyes. "Is that really how you see me?"

"It's not how I see you, Avery. It's how you are. Beautiful, inside and out." I push her long hair back behind her ear and smile at her. "I don't know how I would have managed here without you as my friend."

"Oh!" She tosses her head and waves me away. But she is chewing her lip, and there is something in her eyes that makes me frown.

"Avery," I say gently. "Are you okay?"

"Sure." She turns a brittle smile to me. "Apart from the fact that your brother clearly never liked me at all, and the only other two bachelors in this hokey town are too busy running after you to even notice I exist—sure, Harper. I'm fine."

Two bachelors? I frown, trying to work out what she means.

"Oh, come on, Harper," she says impatiently, reaching into her bag and withdrawing another bottle of champagne that I am too slow to prevent her from opening. "Jeremiah's uncle was back less than a day and he came running to see you. Whatever you say, he has a major thing for you. And Tate was talking to you for most of the night." She tries to smile, but it doesn't quite work. "Couldn't just one of them have wanted me?" The longing in her tone is desolate and forlorn.

I'm not sure what to say, and I can't help but feel relieved when I find Jeremiah lingering in the doorway.

"Avery," he says tentatively, "I've been trying to rehang the lights that have fallen down by the river, but I can't seem to get them right. Is there any chance you'd help me?"

"Fallen down?" Champagne temporarily forgotten, Avery stands up with remarkable stability, her face completely focused. "Do I have to do *everything* myself?" She flounces out of the room. I shoot Jeremiah a grateful look as he follows her, then slump back down on the bed, one arm over my eyes.

All I really want is time to think through how I'm supposed to react to Antoine being here, but something tells me no amount of time would make that any clearer. I glare at the clothes hanging on a makeshift pole that Connor suspended on chains from the ceiling to act as a wardrobe. I haven't even thought about what I'm going to wear. A guilty part of me wonders if anyone would miss me if I simply didn't show. *Perhaps I can just hide up here all night?*

I can't imagine anything worse than pretending to enjoy a party while two deadly monsters slumber beneath us and my vampire husband pretends that I don't exist.

As if to challenge me further, when the afternoon shadows turn to dusk, I come downstairs to find Antoine and Tate stationed on opposite sides of the mansion. Tate is on the front porch talking to Jeremiah. I leave him there and go out back to find Antoine staring down to where fairy lights and trestle tables mark the edge of the party, and beyond them the dock juts out over the slow-moving river.

Instead of ignoring me, Antoine glances at me, taking in my faded jeans, soft pink cotton peasant blouse, and low mules. His mouth turns up on one side in a way that is so unexpected it makes my breath catch and butterflies dance inside. "No dress?" he murmurs, and I know he is referring to the dress I wore last time I went to a party, the night he wound up having to rescue me from the unwelcome attention of a group of men whom he later compelled. That memory brings back others, even more disturbing, and I feel heat rise on my neck.

"The dress didn't work so well for me, last time."

"Oh, I don't know. It seemed to get everyone's attention." I feel his eyes scorch me through the thin stuff of the blouse and stare determinedly down the slope. I don't want to look at him.

"Exactly," I say primly, taking a larger swallow of champagne than is probably wise. "I'd rather not attract that kind of attention again."

"I'd rather you didn't have a party at all."

"Well." I turn and face him before I remember how dangerous it is to do that. "That isn't up to you, now, is it?"

I forgot how his eyes feel, as if they're reaching inside me, to the place where I am unutterably alone and have been ever since Tessa died. The place nobody else ever sees or even senses. A place that has only ever felt warmed by the fire in Antoine Marigny's eyes, by the comfort of his arms around me.

"No, it isn't up to me," he says quietly. Something stirs behind his eyes and for a moment I see a glimpse of the man I knew, enough that everything in me seems to slow down to a heavy, dull pulse. "I'm not sure anything is up to me anymore," he murmurs. Somehow, without me noticing, I've moved closer to him, so only inches separate us. In a swift movement, he takes my hand and raises it to the soft lamp by the door, so the emerald on my finger glows in the dusk. "You still wear it," he says, though he is looking at me, not the ring, when he speaks.

I turn my hand over so his lies on top. His silver wedding band gleams dully beside my emerald.

"So do you."

"Always." His smile is utterly gone, and his eyes on mine are deep as the river below. My skin is fired with a heat that has no place in the fall night. "Harper." His thumb moves gently across my palm, and my hand becomes the center of sensation in my body, acutely sensitive to his touch. His lips part, and suddenly I can't bear to hear what he is about to say next.

"Can we just have tonight?" The words tumble out before I can stop them. He frowns but I race on without waiting for his response. "I know you won't stay." It hurts to say it aloud. "I know you only came back because of the binding." He flinches slightly when I say that, his hand tightening on mine. "But just for one night," I say softly, "can we pretend that you are Jeremiah's young uncle come to visit—and I'm just an ordinary girl hosting a party for her friend?"

"An ordinary girl." He glances down at the Marigny emerald on my finger and his lips curve in a slow smile. "Ordinary is the last word I would use to describe you, Harper."

"But just for tonight, can't we at least try?"

The slow smile grows in a way that makes my heart skip. "And what, do you imagine, ordinary might look like?"

"Well." I hear a car pull up out front, the slamming of doors and clamor of voices. "I can pretend to ignore you across the party, and you can pretend you don't notice me. And every now and then—" I look up to find him watching me with a smile of such warmth I feel the cold place inside me glow—"I will look up to find you watching me."

"And what happens at the end of the night?" His voice is slightly husky, his eyes caress my face, and every inch of skin on the hand he holds is tingling.

"I guess," I say, a little breathlessly, "that we'll just have to wait to find out, won't we?"

And before he can answer I turn inside to greet my guests, trying to ignore the hard length of him barely feet away, and the amused weight of his eyes on my back.

CHAPTER 11

PARTY

*B*y midway through the evening, the party is in full swing, and I'm beginning to feel secretly grateful that both Tate and Antoine are present. I can't help but remember the last party I attended, at Perdu Inlet, and how quickly things had gotten out of control. Avery's bayou friends haven't arrived yet, but there are already plenty of people, and more than enough alcohol. A waxing moon beams down on the river, and the night feels edgy and unpredictable.

"Hey, Harper! Great party. You look hot." It's Jared Baudelaire, the jock whose father owns half the town, and he's smiling at me in a way that suggests he is not only confident in his own desirability, but also in my awareness of it.

"Jared." I greet him cautiously. After my last experience of dressing up at a riverside party resulted in men taking my dress as an open invitation, "hot" is definitely not the reaction I was going for. Discomfort makes me awkward. I know most of the girls at school think Jared's incredibly attractive. I can't see it, but then rarely do I see much in the boys from school. And since Antoine, I don't see anyone, anymore. Just as this passes through my mind, I see Antoine standing on the fringe of the party, lounging against an old oak. One hand is thrust into his jeans pocket and a bottle dangles loosely from the other. He's watching me with a slight smile that says he knows exactly how uncomfortable I feel at Jared's graceless compliment.

His knowing smile goads me just enough that I turn my most dazzling smile on Jared. "So, you play football, huh." I wince at my clumsy attempt at small talk. Jared, however, seems oblivious to my complete lack of social skills and launches eagerly into a long replay of the game he played last weekend. When he starts moving plastic cups around to simulate the play, which in turn draws an avid crowd of his fellow jocks and the girls who admire them, I glance up to find Antoine still watching me. He raises his bottle in an ironic salute and I make a face. His smile grows broader and despite myself, I feel the corners of my mouth twitch. I hate that he can do this, make me laugh when I should be mad. Color heats my cheeks and I look away, hoping he hasn't noticed, but when I glance back he is grinning openly. I shake my head, rolling my eyes upwards. My stomach is doing a strange little dance. His eyes travel slowly across my collarbone, making my skin tingle, then down, resting pointedly on my left hand, where the emerald seems to glow with an inner fire that warms my whole hand. When he looks up he is no longer smiling, and his eyes burn into mine in a way that makes my pulse jump violently. The party continues around us and I am amazed that others can't feel the electricity crackling over the ground between us. Jared forgotten, I begin moving toward Antoine as if guided by a will greater than my own, and his mouth curves in the secret smile that is the man I remember, the man I married in rush of red magnolia.

Then a faint commotion from the river breaks the moment, and just as suddenly the warmth disappears from Antoine's face, leaving only the cold, hard mask he has worn since his return. A group of men leap from a boat they tie to the dock and saunter up the slope. They're burly and seem much older than the rest of the party. In a town as small as Deepwater, parties tend to be cross-aged affairs, ranging from those of college age and above, down to our own high school crowd. These men, though, are altogether different. Their necks and arms are heavily tattooed and muscled. They have hard eyes and look around at the party-goers with a detached, assessing manner that sets them clearly apart. Antoine's eyes narrow as Avery rushes past him toward the newcomers, and there is nothing relaxed about his taut stance as he watches her greet them.

"Remy! You came!" In a tipsy, overly familiar rush of long limbs, Avery throws herself into the arms of a man in a plaid shirt cut off at the shoulders and cargo trousers that have seen better days. His friends, dressed equally roughly, stand behind him, looking as if they are half expecting to be thrown out.

"Honey," the man murmurs, giving Avery a smile that reminds me of a butcher eyeing a particularly juicy cut, "of course we came." I recognize Remy, I realize. He was the driver of the truck I'd seen at the lumberyard months ago, the morning after the party when I'd been attacked. He's got a wicked smile and a gleam in his eye that just screams trouble.

Unfortunately, I'm well aware that lately, trouble seems to be one of Avery's closest friends.

"Harper!" Avery cries, color hectic in her face. "These are the friends I told you about from the bayou." I force down a feeling of unease and offer a welcome that goes largely unacknowl-edged. The bayou men nod briefly to Jared, greet a couple of other boys, and form a small circle of their own company. They drink directly from whiskey bottles, eyeing the girls with lazy, suggestive eyes.

"Interesting company you choose to keep these days, broth-er." I turn in surprise to find Tate, with no trace of his customary smile, standing on one side of me. Antoine is on the other, though I didn't notice him approach. When he answers Tate, his voice is equally hard.

"Had I known anything of their being invited, believe me when I say it would have been stopped."

"What would have been stopped?" Bewildered, I look between them, but when Antoine speaks, he does so in a low voice and without meeting my eyes.

"Harper, go inside and stay there. Take as many people with you as you can."

"Not until you tell me what is going on."

"Harper." His voice is tight. "Please, just do it."

"Even if I could," I say, looking around, "there's no way I can move an entire party inside. There's a hundred or more people here." Even as I speak, the man who hugged Avery looks up the lawn to where we are standing. His eyes narrow as he spots Antoine and Tate, and he murmurs something to the man next to him. A moment later the entire group is looking our way— and not in a friendly manner.

"I'd say it's a little late for escape, brother," murmurs Tate. Antoine glances across me, and a look passes between him and Tate that seems to supersede whatever animosity they feel for each other.

"We get them to the river," murmurs Antoine.

"Agreed," says Tate. They are already moving down the lawn. The men from the bayou, faces hard and unfriendly, watch their approach, moving closer together as if anticipating an attack.

"Avery," I hear Antoine say quietly as he and Tate approach the group. "I think Harper is looking for you."

"Well," Avery counters, in a high-pitched voice that seems to have an edge of hysteria to it, "I'm talking with my friends." She clings tightly to Remy's arm.

"Yeah," Remy says, throwing Antoine an insolent grin. "She's talking with her friends."

Antoine leans forward and murmurs something in the man's ear. Remy's grin disappears abruptly. He drops Avery's arm, taking a step backward and eyeing Antoine and Tate warily.

One of his friends steps forward aggressively, and in a moment Tate is at his side. Perhaps it's only because I know what they are that I see the grip Tate has on the man's arm and sense the iron strength in it, just as I involuntarily wince as Antoine puts a seemingly friendly arm around another of the men, hard enough that the man stumbles.

"Say happy birthday and goodnight to Avery," Antoine says to the man he's holding, the steel beneath his courteous tone unmistakeable. The man looks like he is about to protest when Remy interrupts.

"Do as he says, Henri." Remy folds his arms and meets Antoine's eyes. "I don't fancy finding my boat wrapped around a tree," he says lightly. "Or myself naked and dancing in the middle of the road."

Antoine's mouth twists slightly. "Wise choice."

"Happy birthday, Avery," Henri mumbles, shooting Antoine a resentful glance. "Goodnight."

"Wait!" Avery glares at Antoine. "You can't make my friends leave. I invited them, and it's my party."

"Your *friends*," says Antoine tightly, "aren't supposed to be on this side of the river."

As if emboldened by Avery's outburst, Henri glares at Antoine. "The house was sold," he says roughly, eyeing me with hostility. "It isn't Marigny land anymore." Cold fear runs down my spine, and a strange noise roars in my ears.

Are they vampires?

I look around at the party crowd, still largely oblivious to the drama unfolding in front of them, of the danger they are in. I look at the men and feel the horrible nearness of death, the fragility of everyone here in the face of creatures they cannot begin to imagine.

"Henri." Remy is no longer smiling. "It's time to go."

"I'd listen to your brother, Henri." Antoine smiles coldly. "If it were no longer Marigny land, you would already be dead.

Instead, I and my brother here are doing you the courtesy of allowing you to leave with your lives. I suggest you take that opportunity."

I can't help but notice the ease with which Antoine and Tate seem to operate together, as if they are part of the same machine, fitting together as neatly as any brothers I've met. They may harbour old grudges, I think, but when it comes to it, they are family, just as Connor and I are.

I wonder if they realize that themselves.

"What's going on?" Avery's voice is rising, shrill with fear and the edge of tears. Without thinking, I tumble down the stairs, ignoring Antoine's glowering expression, and take Avery's hand. "Come with me." I force myself to smile. "There's way too much testosterone going on here. Cass and I just found a bottle of rosé that has birthday girl written all over it, and I think we should open it."

"Cass?" Avery stares at me, her face flushed and angry. "Cass and Connor disappeared into that barricaded library as soon as they could get away." Avery looks about wildly, as if searching for an escape, then her face crumples into tears. "I'm sick of all of you," she announces dramatically, her voice shaky and uneven. "Just leave me alone." Grabbing a half-empty bottle from a nearby table, she weaves off unsteadily toward the house.

I let out a breath I didn't realize I was holding. I smile brightly at those nearest me. "We're going to bring the cake out," I say. "It's just inside." There's enough noise that most people haven't noticed much of the disturbance, and they start to move up the slope and flow into the house willingly enough, casting the bayou group no more than curious glances as they pass. I herd them indoors and toward the kitchen, though most remain in the hallway, spilling onto the porch, and plenty of others linger still on the lawn.

I stay at the bottom of the porch stairs, and as the crowd

moves inside, I go toward where Antoine and Tate are still standing with the bayou group. Henri is staring at my hand, and I realize after a moment that he is looking at the emerald.

"I thought there were no more Marignys left." He's frowning, as if he's trying to puzzle something out.

"You thought wrong," says Antoine grimly. He nods at Tate, and somehow the bayou group are suddenly halfway down the slope, heading toward the river. Beneath the wide spread of the red magnolia's branches they stop, shielded by shadow, and the men turn to face Antoine and Tate. I don't need to see or hear them to know the standoff is about to turn into something far more violent. It seems extraordinary to me that the rest of the party is continuing, as if death is not about to reach out into the warm southern night.

I can't stand by and watch. I run toward them—am halfway down the slope toward the dock before I consciously think of what I'm doing. I don't know what I will do when I reach the group in the shadows. I only know that I can't simply stand and passively watch as disaster unfolds.

Then a deathly scream rips the air, and chaos of another kind is unleashed.

CHAPTER 12

UNBOUND

A cold wind whips past me. It's close enough that I shudder, my body sensing danger before my conscious mind registers what it is. People seem to scatter like leaves on the porch behind me, but I don't see what it is that disperses them. I look to Antoine and Tate, only to see them both flung aside as if they were no more than dolls, thrust hard against the trees lining the lawn by the same invisible force that just scattered the party. Beyond them, in the shadows of the trees, the group of men from the bayou slump to the ground in quick succession. I can't see what it is that attacks them. I'm aware of shadows that move too fast to track, a disturbance of the night that is cold and somehow rank. I've felt the same quality of air before, I realize, smelled the same scent—when the cellar was opened, a few months earlier.

Even as I try to process what that means, and my frozen body takes one uncertain step, Tate races past me and into the house as Antoine appears at my side, his face tense and alert. "They're out," he says briefly.

There is no need for him to tell me who *they* are. Somehow, Keziah and Caleb have escaped.

"They're gone," he continues. "Gather as many people as you can. If anyone asks, tell them there was an accident in the cellar. Tate will take care of them." He touches my cheek, a fleeting gesture that I want to grasp and hold on to.

"Where are you going?" But I'm speaking to empty air. Antoine has raced back down the slope to the inert bodies that are fallen among the trees. I see shadows moving but can't make out what's happening. I walk unsteadily toward the stairs.

"Harper!" It's Jared, surrounded by a group from school. "What's going on? Who screamed?" As he asks the question, more people stumble out of the house onto the porch, looking confused. I know that look. Tate is already compelling them.

I summon what I hope is a reassuring smile. "Someone accidentally opened our cellar," I say, as calmly as I can. Lies, I remember from watching some film or other, are always best if they have a basis in truth. "It's dangerous and unstable. Part of the roof has fallen in. But don't worry—we've already sent someone to get them out."

"Well, then we need to call an ambulance, get help." Jared's face darkens, and he turns toward the house, beginning to call orders to his teammates. I can feel the situation escalating, but as Jared heads for the back door, suddenly Tate is there on the porch. He seems larger somehow than his lithe figure, more imposing, and the boys stop in their tracks.

"The situation is under control." Tate uses the low tone I recognize as compulsion. But rather than the intimate, intense way I've seen it done before, Tate's voice seems to project across not only the porch, but the entire slope, drawing partygoers in close to listen. "Nobody was hurt, but the house needs to be evacuated immediately, for everyone's safety. The party will carry on at Jared's house. It's better there, anyway. There's a pool, and Jared's parents are away." Even as he finishes speaking, the crowd begins to drift away, chattering among themselves and piling into cars. Barely ten minutes later, all that is left of the party is a twinkling line of headlights moving down the driveway and plastic beer cups strewn like dead flowers over the grass. A rush of heated air scorches my skin, but I don't even see Antoine's face as I feel him pass by me. I want to reach for him, to hold on, but he is already inside the house, and all I see is a brief glimpse of his tall figure disappearing into the kitchen.

"The men from the bayou?" I ask as Tate comes toward me. I turn to look down the slope, but the bodies I saw fall are no longer there.

"Gone," Tate says briefly. Looking over my shoulder, he moves around me and gestures into the house. "Come inside, Harper. It isn't safe out here."

"Who were those men?" I stop and look at him. "*What* were they, Tate?"

He is about to dismiss me, when his eyes meet mine and he sees I won't let it go. "I will tell you, Harper. But for now, we have more important things to deal with." I'm about to push the issue when Jeremiah appears at the door. His face is ashen.

"Connor and Avery are in the kitchen." He speaks directly to Tate. "Antoine compelled them to stay there." His eyes slide toward me then away again. "Antoine is in the library. With Cass."

Once more, Tate's face seems to grow suddenly older, all the centuries he has lived shadowing his smooth-skinned features. It's a peculiarity I'm beginning to associate with bad news, and this time is no exception. When Tate addresses Jeremiah, there is a resigned note to his voice, as if he already knows the answer to the question he asks. "Is Cass . . . ?"

Jeremiah swallows. He nods, a slight gesture, as if by making it small he can avoid confirming whatever it is Tate refers to.

"Is Cass what?" Dread grips my stomach as I look between them. "Not dead. She can't be dead." I see Selena's face in my mind, imagine trying to tell her that her only daughter is lying dead in my house, killed by demons I've kept a secret from everyone. I turn toward the library.

"You can't go in there," says Tate, moving swiftly to stand between me and the door.

I stare at him. "Get out of my way," I say flatly.

He looks like he will argue, but when he sees my face, his own expression changes to one of understanding. "Cass isn't dead, Harper."

That stops me. I shake my head, confused. "Then what?" I look between him and Jeremiah, but they don't answer. "What's happened to her?" Behind Tate's back, the library door opens and Antoine steps through. In the moment before he closes it, I see Cass's prone form, lying on the floor by the open passageway to the cellar.

"Cass!" I surge forward and collide with the hard wall of Antoine's chest. His arms come around me suddenly and fiercely, and for a moment, all I can think is that I want to stay here forever.

"You're not hurt," he says roughly. His hand cradles the back of my head, one thumb stroking the nape of my neck, as if testing that I am, indeed, whole.

"I'm fine." My lips almost graze the bare skin at his throat. I pull back slightly and look up at him. "But Cass—"

His eyes are the dark, turbulent, almost purple color of a storm, the preternatural color I've seen them assume under high emotion. They shift over my shoulder to where Tate stands.

"Keziah drank from Cass, Harper." It's Tate who speaks from behind me. "She drained her completely, then fed Cass her own blood." He clears his throat. "Then Keziah killed her."

"She killed her?" I can feel the tension in Antoine's body, in the hand that still holds my head, the iron grip of his arm about my waist. "I thought you said Cass isn't dead?"

"Not exactly." Antoine's voice is gravelly. He tilts my face up and his eyes search my face. "But she should be, Harper."

Slow, terrible realization begins to dawn. I become aware that I'm shaking my head, my jaw rubbing frantically against Antoine's hand in mute denial. His eyes are dark as night on mine.

"That decision isn't Harper's to make." Tate is speaking to Antoine, a hard edge to his voice. "Nor is it yours."

Antoine pulls me closer, holding my head against his chest so I can't see his eyes anymore. I feel the vibration of his voice against the top of my head. "They've eaten, Tate. We don't have much time."

"I know that."

I pull back at the odd note of urgency in their voices, in time to see a look pass between them, something I can't quite read. Tate's hostility fades to resignation. "Go, then."

"I can't. Not yet." Antoine looks down at me. "Harper," he says gently. "You should go to Cass."

I try to read his eyes, but a shadow falls over them as his arms fall away from me, leaving me bereft as I turn toward the library. There is blood on his sleeve, I notice, and his shirt is torn. For a moment I wonder what happened by the river, but there is too much else for me to think of to dwell on it long. I pause at the door to the library. "Will you stay, until—" I can't finish the sentence. There is a short silence in which I can almost feel the two of them looking at each other. "Never mind," I mutter. I knew the answer before I asked.

I push open the door to the sight of Cass's body, limp and lifeless, on the floor. Her neck is covered in blood. I fall to her side, searching for the wound, then frown when I can't find one. Her skin beneath the blood is perfectly whole, with no trace of bite marks or savagery. I cradle her against me. There is no pulse, no warmth to her skin. She feels slack and heavy in my arms and I know, the same way I did when I held my mother's hand the day she died and then Tessa's when she fell away from life, that Cass is horribly, irrevocably gone.

Then the body in my arms takes a sudden, gasping breath. Cass lurches upward, pulls from my grasp, and scurries across the floor to curl against the wall, staring wildly about her.

"Where are they?" she gasps. "What happened to me?"

CHAPTER 13

CHOICES

"Cass." Tate is at her side in an instant, speaking in a low, calm voice, holding her eyes. "What do you remember?"

Cass glances around the room, then down at her own body, as if barely believing it's real. "Harper?" Her eyes search for mine.

"It's okay, Cass." I try for what I hope is a reassuring smile. "Tate is going to help you. Aren't you?" I turn to him, terribly aware of Antoine's grave eyes watching me. Tate doesn't answer me directly but instead smiles at Cass, putting his arm comfortingly around her. "The more I understand, the better I can help," he says gently. "Tell us what happened, Cass." I nod encouragingly when she looks at me.

"I remember Avery." Cass's voice quavers as she looks between us. "Avery came in here. She rushed past us. She was upset, crying. I tried to talk to her but she wouldn't listen. She did something to the bookshelf, and it opened." Her brow furrows and she glances toward where the bookshelf hangs open, the dark opening to the cellar yawning beyond. "She went down that passage." Cass's voice is unsteady. "Connor and I were calling to her, trying to get her to come back up, then something—came out." Her face screws up, and one hand goes to her neck. "It hurt," she whispers, staring at her blood-covered hand. "It hurt so much." She frowns, bewildered. "I think somebody made me drink something, and it tasted awful, like—old blood. And then . . . I don't really remember anything. Nothing at all." Her eyes cut to me. "Why would I have been drinking blood? What came out of the cellar? I thought it was a woman, but it wasn't, and Avery . . ." her voice trails off and she looks around frantically. "Where's Avery? Is she—" she stops, unable to finish the sentence.

"Avery is fine," Antoine says from behind me. The odd note in his voice is still there, a strange tension I can hear, even through his efforts at gentleness with Cass.

"What's wrong with me?" Cass looks around at us, her voice small. "I feel so strange."

Antoine crouches in front of her. "The creatures that came out of the cellar were vampires." Tate tenses, but at a look from Antoine, doesn't say anything. "They drank your blood, Cass. When you were drained completely, one of the vampires, the woman you remember, fed you her own blood." He meets her eyes steadily. "Then she broke your neck."

She stares at him. "But if she broke my neck," she says, her voice quavering, "I would be . . . dead." She hesitates before the last word, as if she realizes how crazy it sounds. Her eyes slide to me. "Harper?" There is enough uncertainty in her voice to break my heart. "What's going on?"

I kneel beside Antoine and take her hand. "You're changing, Cass," I say quietly. It isn't until I say the words aloud that I realize a part of me has known the truth since the moment I knew Cass had been attacked. "You're becoming a vampire." I look at Antoine, but I don't need his faint nod to know I'm right.

"A vampire?" Cass stares at us blankly. "But they're not real."

Tate doesn't smile. "Unfortunately," he says quietly, "vampires are very real, Cass. But you aren't a vampire. Not yet."

"What do you mean? What am I, then?" She looks between us, confused and scared.

I realize both Tate and Antoine are waiting, leaving the decision of how much to tell Cass in my hands. I take a deep breath.

"You have a choice, Cass." I force myself to hold my friend's eyes, just as I hold her hand in mine. I glance at Antoine. "That is right, isn't it? She has a choice?"

Antoine's mouth tightens.

"Yes." Tate's voice is low and pained. "She has a choice." But I can see the warning in Antoine's eyes. I know the choice isn't one anybody should ever have to make.

"Connor." Cass looks around, her eyes wild and afraid, and when I see the pale red edging around her eyeballs, I feel a tremor of fear. Already there is something preternatural in her movements, an inhuman swiftness that's all too familiar to me. "I need to see him, to tell him—"

"You can't." Antoine's voice is calm but firm. "At least, not until you have decided what you will do."

"Decided?" Cass echoes, clearly unable to take in what he means. I cast Antoine a sharp look.

"You must drink human blood." I wince at the words. "To become a vampire. But if you don't want to . . ." Antoine frowns at me, and my voice trails off.

"If you don't drink, Cass," Tate says gently, "then you will die."

Cass's eyes flare, and I try not to cringe from the savagery and pain in their depths. "If you don't want this—" I swallow, the words almost impossible to say "—you will die here. Connor will never know that you survived today, that you faced a choice." I meet Antoine's eyes, feeling a rush of anger that my friend should be in such an impossible, hideous position, unable to help feeling angry at him. "That's right, isn't it? If she chooses to die, she will die here and now?"

Tate looks away from my anger, his face sad and resigned, but Antoine nods curtly. His face is blank, the mask in place again, and he doesn't try to touch me. "Yes," he says simply. He meets Cass's eyes. "I am sorry, Cass. I know it is a terrible choice. But we don't have a lot of time to consider the options." The tension is harder in his voice now, his entire body strung like tight wire, as if he's holding himself there with great effort. "The creatures who made you have escaped. They must be caught, and every moment you remain like this, you are in danger—and so are those around you. You need to make a decision."

"You mean I need to choose whether I live or die?" She stares around at us, her eyes wild. "Now? How am I supposed to make a decision like that?"

Antoine grips her, not gently. "Because if you do not, Cass, we will be forced to make it for you." His tone is so grim she stills under his touch.

"You," she whispers, her eyes moving between Antoine and Tate. "Both of you are vampires?" They nod. "And if I say I don't want this, you're going to kill me?"

Again Antoine nods, not flinching from her eyes. "I will do it myself, Cass. If I don't, you will hurt someone. Even though you won't want to—you will. I can't take that chance."

Something seems to snap into focus in Cass's mind. Her eyes gain an odd clarity, and she turns to me. "Then I want to speak with my mom." Her voice is stronger. "And with Connor. I can't make a decision like this without talking with them first."

"You can't—" begins Antoine.

"She can talk to Connor and Avery, at least," I interrupt, glaring at him. I know it's unfair to blame him, but I feel so angry I can't help it. "All these secrets—what have they achieved? The worst has happened now. The cellar is open. Keziah and Caleb are gone. They broke the binding, and now they've killed my friend. What can possibly be worse than that?"

"Harper." Antoine's fists ball tightly, as if it's taking all his strength not to explode. "You have absolutely no idea how much worse it can get."

"Maybe not." I'm angry too. "But our friends are involved now. Whether you like it or not, they have a right to know. My *brother* has a right to know." I look at Jeremiah, who's been hovering in the doorway.

"I think she's right." He shrugs slightly under Antoine's scrutiny. "I don't like seeing Connor compelled. I didn't like it the last time, either. It isn't fair. Avery opened that cellar. Until Keziah and Caleb are caught, she's in danger, too. They both have a right to know."

"What does he mean, *compelled?*" Cass looks at me in confusion. "What's he talking about?"

I raise my eyebrows at Antoine and he makes an impatient noise. "This is a mistake," he says grimly. "One we don't have time for."

"Let her tell her friends." Tate glances at Antoine then back at me. "But not her mother, Harper. That is impossible."

"If it were up to me," Antoine says tightly, "I wouldn't tell any of them." But to my surprise he doesn't argue with Tate. Instead he stands up and goes to the kitchen, where I hear him speaking in a low voice to Avery and Connor.

"Compulsion is a form of mind control." I stroke the hair back from Cass's face, trying not to notice how odd she feels under my touch or the hectic, unnatural light in her eyes. "It's a —gift—that vampires have. They can erase memories, compel you to believe something is true." I can see Cass trying to absorb it.

"If I die," she says, looking at me, "they will compel everyone to think it was an accident, won't they?" I nod reluctantly. "And nobody will know the truth. My mother. They won't let her see me. She'll never know what happened to me."

"No." It hurts to say the word. "And you can't see her, Cass, not even to say goodbye." I know there is no choice now but honesty, no matter how painful. "If everyone is to believe the lie, you will have to die here, in this room, tonight."

"You mean I can't leave, in case someone sees me."

I nod, my heart breaking at the bewilderment in her face. Then the door opens and Connor is standing there, his face a picture of disbelief. Avery is behind him, and despite my fury at her for opening the cellar door, the grief on her face is so palpable, I find myself rushing to hug her as Connor falls to his knees beside Cass.

"I'm so sorry," Avery sobs over my shoulder. "I'm so sorry, Cass. I didn't mean to let them out. I didn't even know what I was doing."

Behind her, Antoine looks at Tate, and this time I see something I really don't understand, almost a pleading expression. Tate goes to him and they speak in a low tone. "Noya left this morning," I hear Antoine say over the sound of Avery's sobs.

What has Noya got to do with any of this? I think, frowning. Realizing he spoke too loudly, Antoine's eyes meet mine, his expression a cross between apology and grim resolution. Jeremiah, seeing my face, gently removes Avery from my arms, murmuring to her as I move toward Tate and Antoine.

"I have to go," Antoine says again, and this time I recognize the odd note in his voice for what it is—desperation.

"I know," Tate says quietly. "The question is, brother—what will you do?"

"I'll do what has to be done." Antoine's tone is hard and bitter. "As I always have." His eyes rest on me, something rich and heartbreaking in their depths, then shift back to Tate. "Take care of her." His voice is oddly resonant, almost like it contains an echo.

Tate's eyes flare with a strange, indigo blue iridescence, like an oil slick across water. He nods.

Antoine eyes touch my face again, as if he's imprinting it on his memory. I take a half step forward and put my hand out, but I'm too late.

Antoine is already gone.

Filled with foreboding and a dreadful suspicion, I move as if pulled by something beyond myself, running into the kitchen, suddenly certain that if I don't seize this moment, I may never have another one. "Antoine!" He halts where the kitchen gives way to the front porch, his back to me. "Wait."

He turns. "Go back to your friends, Harper." His face is closed and hard.

I take a step forward, then another, until I stand directly in front of him. He leans slightly back, but he doesn't move away. "What did Tate mean?" I try to read his eyes, but they are shuttered, the mask in place. "What is the choice you have to make?"

"Don't ask questions if you don't want their answer." His voice is as cold as his eyes. "You know what has to be done, Harper."

"I know what has to be done to Keziah and Caleb, yes." My words trip over each other. "I know you're hunting them, that you must bind or . . . kill them." I force myself to say the words. "That isn't the choice I'm asking about."

Antoine's eyes narrow slightly.

"I mean after that. After they're caught. What happens then?" I feel the color rushing into my face, and I'm helpless to stop it. "Will you—that is, where will you go?" My voice trails off, and I stare awkwardly at my feet, wishing I knew how to ask what I need to know in a more sophisticated way. I can feel his eyes on me, but I'm too self-conscious to meet them.

"If I hunt Keziah and Caleb down," Antoine says in a low

voice, "and somehow manage to—defeat them, there will be no reason for you and Connor to ever have anything to do with all of this again." I feel my heart clench, so painfully I can barely swallow, and I keep my eyes carefully on the floor. "That is why what happens with Cass is vital, Harper." There's an urgency to his tone that makes me look up. "Do you understand?" I can hear just how raw his voice is, see the cracking of his composure in the rigid set of his jaw, the tension in his body. "Cass drank Keziah's blood," he says roughly. "If she transitions, she will be forever tied to Keziah. And that will mean you and Connor will be forced to remain a part of this world. You will never escape it, Harper. You will never be free of this. Of them."

I force myself to hold his eyes. "You mean that *you* will never be free of this." I keep my voice steady with an effort. He frowns but does not contradict me. "You will never be free of me." I stand in front of him, staring at his eyes, waiting for him to say something, anything, that will tell me I am wrong.

But his eyes are dark as a night sea, and he neither reaches for me nor takes a step in my direction.

"Of all the things I've learned since I met you, never once have I truly believed you to be a monster." Hurt cracks my voice open and fills my eyes with tears I am too proud to let him see me shed, so I turn away. "You might be prepared to sacrifice Cass in order to free yourself." The words rasp in my throat. "But she is my friend. And my brother loves her. I will never let her die, just to help you run to freedom. I'm going to do everything I can to see that she drinks before dawn, Antoine—no matter what it means for you."

His presence behind me is like a magnet drawing me toward him. It takes everything I have to keep my back turned. I know I should walk away, but a traitorous part of me hopes still, against all sense, that he will reach for me. That he will pull me in hard against him and promise me that everything I've just said is wrong, that despite everything I know to be true, he loves me

and wants to stay, not because he is bound to, or from obliga-
tion, but because he truly desires to be at my side.

There is a moment when I could swear I feel him reach out,
come so close I can almost sense his breath on my neck. Then
there is a sudden rush of air, and I turn, knowing even as I do
that Antoine is gone, and I am alone in the still southern night.

CHAPTER 14

TRUTH

I wait in the kitchen until I get my tears under control, splashing cold water on my face and over my guilt. A broken heart seems a petty sideshow when Cass is trying to choose whether to live or die.

When I return to the library, Cass is clinging to an ashen-faced Connor. My brother looks up as I enter, and what I see in his face makes me physically recoil. The last time I saw that empty, haunted look in his eyes was when Tessa was dying and in the sickening days following her death. The thought that I am responsible for making him look like that again breaks me, deep inside.

"You knew something was down there." There's so much hurt and betrayal in his voice that I can do nothing but nod. "Jeremiah said you married Antoine to keep that cellar closed."

I glance at Jeremiah, who shrugs. "I told him."

I nod again. I guess there's no point any longer in keeping secrets. Connor's eyes fall to the ring on my hand. "That never belonged to Mom." His voice is flat and hard, his words a statement of fact rather than a question.

"No."

I can't look at Cass. I remember the day she mentioned the ring to me, weeks ago, when we were by the dock, and the way I brushed her off. Now she not only knows I lied to her, but she's paying with her own life for the consequences of my actions. I twist the ring on my finger and look away, ashamed and heartsick.

Connor is still staring at me. "If your name on that deed sealed the cellar closed, Harper, then how did whatever was in there get out?" Connor looks narrowly at Avery, who is sitting between Tate and Jeremiah, head down so her hair hides her face. "What did you do, Avery?"

I shake my head wearily. "It isn't her fault, Connor. Keziah uses mind control. That's what happened, Avery, isn't it?" I think back to Avery's odd behavior over recent weeks, the visits to Witch Way. "What did she ask you to do?" I take Avery's hand. "It's okay. You can tell us. The more we know, the better we can manage this."

"Oh, we can? And what, exactly, is it that we're managing, Harper?" Connor's anger is palpable. Tate puts a hand on his arm and Connor shakes it off. He subsides, though he's still glaring at me.

Avery looks between Tate and me, then at Cass, who is curled into Connor as if he can somehow shield her from the decision she knows is coming. Avery's face crumples. For a moment I think she will cry again. I feel a particularly uncharitable urge to slap her out of self-pity. The desire must show on my face, because Avery bites her lip, takes a breath, and starts to speak.

"At first, I didn't remember what happened last time the cellar opened." One hand plucks at a stray thread on her top, worrying at it. "I dreamed of it, but I thought that's all it was— bad dreams. Maybe a hangover from the weed I put in the cookies we ate, you know?" She glances guiltily at Connor. "But then, when I came back here the next time, the whispers started. And every time I visited, they just got worse and worse. I didn't want to come here, but it was like I couldn't help myself. I found myself coming every chance I got, finding excuses to turn up, and every time I did the voice got louder. It got so bad I could hear that woman's voice even when I wasn't in the house."

Tate nods. "When Keziah escaped last time, she drank your blood. Even if you don't remember it, it's likely she made you drink hers, too. Blood exchange creates a bond. And you are Natchez, part of the bloodline that bound her. The connection was already potent. By exchanging blood, she made sure you were bound to her beyond any ability to fight the connection."

"She drank my blood?" Avery stares around at us, but when she realizes we aren't going to answer her, she just shudders and goes on. "I could feel her, inside me, around me, like a cold mist. Her whispers became so strong I couldn't remember clearly what was me and what was her." She glances guiltily at Cass. "It was the whispers in my head that told me to go to your shop and search for a wooden box. She described it to me. I found it eventually, underneath a tray of old pendants made out of wood and bone."

"Avery." Tate's gentle manner is abruptly gone, and he grips Avery's hand tightly. "What was inside the box?"

"She told me to look for two special pieces of jewelry." Avery looks around at us nervously. "I kept telling her that I couldn't do it, that your mom would grow suspicious, Cass, but Keziah wouldn't let me give up. I had to pretend I actually wanted to buy those ugly rings, then distract your mom so I could steal the box. Finally I got it, yesterday, before the party. It took so long to pry open. The pieces were in the box, just like she said they would be. One was a bone pendant. It was ugly, like a snake, with a strange face in the center of the curve. The other was made of bone too, I think. It was a ring, with the same pattern carved into it."

"And you took these talismans." When she nods, Tate sits back, his face grave. "And now? Where are they?"

"She has them. Keziah. When she made me open the cellar, she took them." Avery's face is a picture of guilt. I get the feeling there's more to the story, but I don't want to push Avery, who already looks like she wishes the floor would open beneath her.

With a muffled curse, Tate pulls out his phone and turns away. "They have their talismans," he murmurs. I know he's talking to Antoine. He moves away until I can't hear him anymore. I'm not sure whether that's a good thing or not.

Avery turns apologetic eyes to me. "It's like a bad dream. The same as last time." I grasp her hand, about to tell her it isn't her fault, when Connor turns to us, haunted eyes burning with anger.

"You told us to come in here." He throws the words brutally at Avery. "You gave us a bottle of champagne and said we had your blessing, and then you opened the door to the library and told us to enjoy ourselves."

"I didn't mean to." Avery's voice catches in a sob. "It was Cass she wanted. She told me Cass had to be there."

Something fierce flashes in Cass's eyes. "You planned this?" *Is it my imagination, or are they becoming more intensely red?* I glance at Tate and see him watching Cass warily as he puts away his phone. "Cass," he says gently, "it's alright. It isn't Avery's fault." When Connor opens his mouth to object, Tate turns his gaze on my brother. "Avery's story is important." He holds Connor's eyes, his voice low and intense. "We need to hear it."

I should feel guilty that he's compelling my brother, but I don't. We need to know what happened. There's no time for Connor's anger, no matter how justified, and I'm glad when he subsides. Cass glares at Avery. "Go on, then." Her voice is sharp, goading, nothing like the gentle, loving Cass I know. "Tell your story."

"I couldn't help it." Avery glances at the yawning darkness

behind the bookcase, fear washing over her face. "The voice was so strong. It was like a loudspeaker in my head, telling me what to do. I brought the jewelry to the library and acted like I was drunk and upset. You laughed at me." She glances at Connor and despite everything that's happened, I wince at the hurt in her eyes. "I opened the bookcase and walked downstairs. Then I just touched the door." She frowns. "I said something, but I don't remember what it was. The voice whispered the words to me. I just said them." She shakes her head. "And then it was open, and those two—things—were out. It happened so fast I barely remember it. Something took the jewelry pieces from my hand and pushed me down. I think I might have passed out for a moment. When I came upstairs, I found Cass on the floor. Since then . . . nothing. No voices. They've just—stopped." She looks at Cass as if truly seeing her for the first time. "Cass—what's wrong with your eyes? You look different." She breaks off, her own eyes widening as Cass makes a noise in the back of her throat, somewhere between a snarl and a hiss. Cass's face is fierce and savage, and for one horrible moment I think she will tear Avery's head from her shoulders. She looks capable of it. Avery shrinks away from her, biting her lip, shooting me a troubled glance.

Connor, still cradling Cass close to his body, glares at Tate and me.

"Antoine told us Cass was attacked by them," he says slowly, looking between us. "But it's more than that, isn't it? Why did those things tell Avery to make sure Cass was here when they escaped? What exactly is happening to her?"

I realize that Antoine left out the most important part on purpose. He wanted to leave the final choice of how much to say in Cass's hands.

"Cass?" I meet her eyes, letting the question hang in her name on the air. For a long moment it seems the night crackles with waiting as Cass watches me. I can see it all rolling through her mind, can almost hear the impossible futures she faces clash unbearably before her.

Death. Immortality.

Her life ends here, tonight, or goes on forever.

She tells them, and tries to live, or Tate compels Connor and Avery to go—and she dies.

The air is still for a long moment, and then Cass jerks away from Connor and looks around the room.

"I don't know why it had to be me." Her voice is hard and clear. "But whatever the reason—I'm dead, Connor." Her voice chokes on the final word, but her eyes are like lasers, pinning each of us in turn. She ignores Avery and Connor's shock and goes on. "The thing gave me its blood before it killed me. And now I'm in transition."

"In transition?" Connor stares at her. Avery has been stunned into silence. "Transition to what?"

Cass's eyes shift to me, and I know she can't bring herself to say it.

"The creatures in the cellar," I say quietly. "Keziah and Caleb. They're vampires."

"Vampires," Connor says flatly. "We've been living with vampires in our cellar." He stares at me. "And you knew. All this time, you knew." I can't find the words to answer him. He turns to Cass. "What will happen?"

"If I don't drink human blood before dawn," Cass says in a voice that sounds like glass about to break, "I will die when the sun comes up."

She has barely finished speaking when Connor holds out his arm. Before any of us can say anything he cuts it with his pocket knife, so blood falls in bright drops to the dusty floor. "Drink, then," he says simply.

"Connor!" I move toward him, but the look he gives me is so savage it stops me in my tracks.

"It isn't that simple." Tate is at Connor's side, wrapping cloth around the cut, but not before I see Cass's eyes flare, the sudden parting of her lips as she stares at the blood on the floor. Tate moves behind Cass, his hands resting gently on her shoulders as he faces the rest of us. Perhaps it's only me who understands the strength in those hands, the fact that Tate's hold is not only one of reassurance, but one of restraint. "Cass doesn't just need to drink human blood. She needs to drain a human, to their death." Seeing the incomprehension on our faces, Tate sighs.

"She has to kill someone," he says bluntly. "In order to transition to immortality, Cass must take a life herself."

Connor stares at him. "And if she doesn't? If she just drinks enough blood to—survive?"

I can see the sympathy in Tate's eyes. "She will not exist long," he says quietly. I can clearly see that there's more to it and just as clearly that he doesn't want to elaborate.

"What does that mean—she won't exist for long?" The gaps in Tate's words aren't lost on Connor either, obviously. "What aren't you saying?"

Tate glances at me.

"Don't look at Harper," snaps Connor. "If you've got more to say, then say it."

I nod slightly in Tate's direction. No matter how ugly the truth, I know truth is the only way forward. Tate stiffens, as if bracing himself for what he has to say.

"If Cass does what you suggest, she will become a cursed creature, neither alive nor dead. Something that lives in the shadows, and only for blood, until she goes insane. She may exist for a time, so long as she constantly drinks blood, but the lust for it will consume her, until every shred of her humanity is lost. She will eventually kill not one person, but hundreds. Her body will waste away, unable to consume the food her human form needs, for it is dead, yet incapable of surviving on blood, as our kind do. By then, it will be too late for her to gain immortality." His voice is gentle but remorseless. "Her second end will come slowly and horribly, and long before it happens, you will beg me to find her and burn her, for that is the only way to end such suffering." He turns to Cass and speaks directly to her. "Unless you take a life before dawn and transition the right way, you will never truly be immortal. That's why you need to make your choice quickly."

His words stretch like a grotesque landscape before us. I can't look at Cass or Connor.

"You." Connor is staring at Tate. "And Antoine. How do you know all of this?"

Tate meets his eyes steadily. "I think you already know the answer to that," he says quietly.

I wait for Connor to look at me, but he doesn't. He's holding Cass close, stroking her hair, the two of them staring at one another as if there is nobody else in the room, their grief and horror palpable.

I'm aware of Avery, still and horrified beside me, and then her voice cuts into the silence. "I'll do it." Her voice is quavering but determined. "I did this. It's me who should die, Cass. Not you."

"Avery—" I put out my hand, but stop when Connor leaps to his feet, his face white and angry.

"If it were my choice," he says to Avery, his voice shaking, "I'd open your throat myself." He turns to me and I flinch at the betrayal and confusion in his eyes. "And as for you," he says bitterly, "you had Antoine use mind control on me, didn't you? So I would forget whatever I saw down there. That's why I was always so confused when I thought about the cellar. Isn't it?"

"It's compulsion." Jeremiah meets Connor's eyes, red-faced. "The mind control. It's called compulsion."

"You knew about this?" Connor stares at Jeremiah in disbelief. "And you let her hold a party here?" His voice rises as he turns back to me. "You *married* one of them, Harper! How could you do that?"

"I'm sorry, Connor." It's all I can think of to say.

"Sorry?" He stares at me disbelievingly. "Is that all you've got, Harper? Seriously?" His eyes swivel to Jeremiah, who meets them with a resigned expression, guilt and defiance warring in his face. "And you," Connor says slowly. "I thought we were friends. But you must have known about this, even back when your parents sold the house, and yet you did nothing."

"That isn't true," I protest. "You don't know the whole story, Connor."

"I don't need to." Connor cuts me off curtly. "I don't need to hear any more of your lies." He turns his back on us and draws Cass close to him again. "Just leave Cass to make this decision without any of you telling her what to do." He holds her face and speaks just to her, his voice softening. "I can leave too, if you want it that way." There is such pain in his voice, so much grief, I feel my own heart crack open again, worse perhaps than it ever was with Tessa or Mom.

This death is *my* fault. It isn't cancer, or kidney disease, or any human frailty that caused it. Cass is dying because I thought I could find a way around a centuries-old magical curse. She's dying because I couldn't face leaving Antoine.

She's dying because of my selfish decisions, and I have no right to stand at her side as she makes her choice.

Cass grips his hand in a wordless plea. Connor covers it with his own.

One by one we turn and leave the library. The last thing I see before I close the door behind us is Cass wrapped in Connor's arms, her red-rimmed eyes terrified and accusing as she watches me over his shoulder.

CHAPTER 15

BONDS

J'm standing on the front porch, staring out into the night that so recently swallowed Antoine, when Tate comes to stand beside me.

"I've tried to call Noya a hundred times." I stare into the darkness. "The calls go straight to voicemail."

"Are you really surprised by that?"

I shrug. "I guess I just hoped she meant it when she gave me her number and told me I could call her anytime."

"Antoine tried to call her the moment this happened. I've sent messages. She hasn't answered any of them."

I nod. He waits.

"I have questions," I say after a moment.

"I know."

I can hear Jeremiah and Avery talking in the kitchen behind me, the sound of Avery crying softly. I know that I should be in there, comforting her. But it isn't her fault. It's mine. Even if Avery doesn't fully realize that yet, Cass certainly does, not to mention Connor. I feel his shock and betrayal as if it were my own, and if I turn from it, I see Cass. Her red-rimmed eyes are burned into my mind, right beside the memory of Antoine's face when he said that if Cass died, he would have no reason to return.

"Antoine doesn't want Cass to complete the transition." I speak without looking at Tate. "With Keziah and Caleb out, there's nothing holding him here—he can hunt them down and try, at least, to destroy them. If he succeeds, he can leave, cut the ties with his past. But if Cass turns, it becomes more complicated. He can't just walk away and leave her here, not knowing what she might do, who she might place in danger. He will be stuck here when what he really wants is to be done with it. With all of this."

"With you," says Tate softly, finishing the sentence I can't bring myself to. I nod and swallow the pain in my chest.

A short silence falls, filled with the heavy weight of the decision lying half dead in the house behind us and the pain left by Antoine's departure. "Avery can't sacrifice herself," I say in a low voice to Tate.

"Of course she can't." I'm more relieved than I want to admit by Tate's immediate agreement. "And there's more to it," he continues, his voice equally low. "Things I don't want to say to Cass until she's made her choice." Tate glances over my shoulder and leads me off the porch, into the shadows of the magnolia. "Transition is more than simply draining a human of blood, Harper. The first human we take is not just a life force. They become part of us, sealed indelibly into our form, bound into our immortality. We absorb them, merge with them. That life changes us forever." His face is troubled in the moonlight, dappled by the magnolia branches as he looks at me.

"What do you mean?" I'm both horrified and fascinated. "That you somehow become the person you kill?"

"In a way, yes." Tate pauses, gauging my reaction, then goes on. "Aspects of their personality become ours. Their gifts, their flaws. We absorb it all. We are no longer what we were. We become something else. And our Maker—the vampire who

gives us their blood, who creates the transition in our bodies—
we're forever connected to them, too, though in a different
way."

"Connected how?"

Tate shrugs. "The bond is felt by the vampire, rather than the
Maker themselves, though a Maker can use it to manipulate the
vampire. The nature of it depends. The bond is different in
every case. Sometimes it's an acute awareness of what the
Maker is feeling. In others it is a mirroring, where the vampire
behaves as their Maker does. There are those who share a bond
of obedience, and still others who share a bond of unbreakable,
mutual love. Much depends upon the relationship between
Maker and vampire at the time of transition. In almost all cases,
both can track the other, or at the very least, have an awareness
of the other's proximity."

"Antoine made you." I frown. "What is your bond with him
like?"

"We were as brothers, before I was made," he says quietly.
"That bond deepened." His mouth twists. "At least, it did for me.
I wanted to hate Antoine. I tried to, for many years. But I
couldn't. Not then and not now. It is both my gift, and my curse,
that I cannot cease caring for him. We cannot break the bond
with our Maker, no matter how we might wish to. It is what it
is. Until one of us meets our end, we are bound."

"And the first person you—drank?" I search his face, but he
has retreated subtly into the shadows, and I can no longer read
his eyes. "Who was it? What were they like?"

"He was a soldier." Tate's voice is oddly dispassionate. "Louis
Marais. A white man, French, who had no conscience. He took
pride and pleasure in murdering my people, as he did in abusing
the slaves on nearby properties. His savagery in battle was
legend, his sins tolerated by his peers because of his deadly
skills. I had known him, and hated him, in my human life. I
thought that by killing him I was ridding the world of a

monster. I didn't know, then, that the monster he was would become part of me. Not even Antoine himself understood that, at the beginning. There were none of our kind to teach us. Both of us learned alone, and by experience, until the years brought us in contact with others of our kind to learn from."

I try and fail to imagine Tate as a killer, a monster. He is so gentle and kind, it is impossible. "But you didn't become a murderer," I say. "You are as far from being a monster as I can imagine."

"Perhaps now. But at the start—" he breaks off, shaking his head. "I was already consumed by rage over what Antoine had done to me. Marais's nature found fertile ground in my anger. I became more deadly than even Keziah and Caleb had been." He looks away from me, his voice roughening. "I massacred an entire garrison of Frenchmen, an atrocity that made it into history books and is still spoken of today. The attack was blamed on a renegade band of my own people, and the retribution taken against them was savage and swift. Members of my own family paid with their lives for my insanity." I can hear the tension and old pain in his voice. "I didn't care. I was too driven by bloodlust and fury to do anything but kill and keep killing. It was many years before I learned to live with the warrior in my blood, to accept his gifts and tame his darker impulses." He swallows, taking a deep breath before continuing. "Eventually I came to peace, came even to appreciate the insights I gained from absorbing him. My own talents as a diplomat, the negotiator for my people, were enhanced by the understanding of white men's thinking the soldier had given me. I realized I could understand the newcomers in a way none of my people had before, could see the world from their perspective as much as from my own." His face is tired. "It is an understanding that has proven both blessing and curse over the centuries."

His words paint images that make my mind whirl, questions

and realisations moving like pieces of a jigsaw in the confusion. I try to absorb what he is saying, to make sense of it, but the full picture remains elusive.

"You haven't asked," Tate says gently. "But I know you want to. What is the nature of Antoine's bond with Keziah? And what was Atsila like, my mother, the person who merged with Antoine when he was made?"

I nod, grateful he didn't make me ask the questions aloud, both desperate to hear the answers and afraid of what I might learn.

"You must remember that my tribe made Antoine to be their weapon." Tate's eyes are dark. "He was created to kill the monsters they feared would destroy them all. My people tried to give him every advantage, to make him the most potent creature they could. My mother may not have known anything of vampires, but she had an innate understanding of the power of blood sacrifice, and she knew how to use such power wisely. Not only did my mother seal the sun into Antoine's flesh. She sealed it with the greatest sacrifice our tribe could offer—that of her own life. She was the oldest, wisest medicine woman in our tribe, wife to the Great Sun and herself a daughter of another Great Sun. She was both honorable and compassionate. Some might say, honorable to a fault." He smiles at me. "It isn't always easy, to be loved by those who put honor before anything else. My mother was such a person. She didn't think of herself or her children first, but only ever for what the noble course would be, the road that would best serve others.

"She wanted to grant Antoine the benefit of her wisdom and experience, gift him the magic and nobility that flowed through her veins. She may not have known how the first sacrifice acts in those of our kind, but she knew enough of magic to know the power inherent in blood sacrifice and to hope her sacrifice would help him."

"Did it work?" I need to know, to understand who he

became. I want to know who the man is that I am so bound to, that I cannot forget, no matter how I sometimes wish I could.

Tate's face darkens. "In a fashion. Antoine became the most potent creature of our kind, just as my people had hoped and my mother planned. She bound the sun into his body with the totem of the treaty, then as dawn broke, gave herself to him. He rose with the sun, gleaming with light, almost shining with power."

I remember the first day I saw him, in the parking lot at school, the way he had seemed to radiate vitality and life, as if he was simply *more* than any other person there. Even from across the lot, I had felt the impact of his eyes, known their color and the shape of his body. I had felt his power, even then.

"But the power did not belong to him alone," Tate went on. "My mother knew nothing of the Maker's bond. She hadn't realized Keziah could use her bond with Antoine to compel him, to make him her servant. None of us realized that the weapon we had sacrificed everything to make could also become a tool used against us. By the time we realized what we had done, Antoine was Keziah's slave, forced to do her will instead of the one task he had been created for: killing Keziah and Caleb. Before he transitioned, Antoine hated Keziah. But he feared her, too—the control she had over his family, what she might still do to him. During the time in which he had been drinking her blood, she had already played on both the hate and the fear to control him. She had intended to turn him eventually, remember. She intentionally built the bond between them, hoping, I imagine, to make it one of complete obedience when the time came."

I am trying to absorb this, what it means, even now, for Antoine.

"But he must have overcome it," I say. "He managed to contain them, after all, to help bind them into the cellar."

"Antoine was never supposed to bind them." Tate meets my

eyes. "The binding was only ever intended to be a temporary measure, something to trap them until we could work out how they could be killed. As soon as we did, Antoine was supposed to kill them. It was only after he was made that it became obvious that he would never be strong enough to resist Keziah long enough to kill her, even if we could find a way to do it."

I digest this for a moment. "That's why he trapped himself inside with them." It was something I never understood before: why Antoine had felt the need to die alongside those who created him. "He couldn't kill her, but he wouldn't allow himself to become her weapon, either."

Tate nods. "There was a war within him, in the days after he transitioned. Keziah played on the ruthless loner he had been, the wounded, angry man she had witnessed reject his family and society itself. But as strong as Keziah was, my mother, with all her wisdom, honor, and compassion, was strong, too. Antoine had been badly affected by the cruelty of his family. He had become an island, a man who needed no one. In his transition, both parts of him became amplified: the lone wolf, abandoned and angry—and the man of honor, who loved his sister, knew me as a brother, and felt a kinship with the Natchez people he never had with his own.

"Keziah whispered that without her, he would forever be alone. She promised the warrior in him war and savage invincibility. But if Antoine the lone wolf was hungry to follow Keziah's promises of blood, the honorable man within him clung to my mother's nobility and fought back. He wrestled Keziah's compulsion in secret, until he found the strength to rise above her influence for long enough to trap all three of them in that cellar. Antoine was almost insane by then, rent in two by the conflicting loyalties in his heart."

"He never told me that." I pluck mindlessly at a stray leaf on the branch above. "When Jeremiah told me about his transition, he made it seem like it all happened in one day, that Antoine transitioned, then captured Keziah and Caleb immediately after."

"Antoine has never spoken of that time. Not to me, not to anyone. I'm certain he never relayed it in the family history. I sometimes think he's spent most of the past three centuries trying to forget it." Tate looks at me soberly. "You asked me once how I can bear to be near Antoine, after what he did to me. And I told you not to think me blameless. I am not. I didn't just encourage Antoine to sacrifice himself in his sister's place—I would have killed him myself if he hadn't." He grimaces. "I was remorseless, ruthless. I'd have done anything to save Marguerite. Antoine knew that. And when he did what I'd asked of him, he didn't just lose his life, Harper. He lost his free will. And his sanity."

I think back to Antoine telling me of the choice he'd made. "I don't think he sees it the same way," I say softly. "I don't think Antoine blames you for his choice. I think he would have made it anyway."

Tate smiles grimly. "You can think that, if you wish. But I know the truth."

"And now?" I think of Antoine as he left me, and a terrible dread seizes my chest. "If he can't bind her or kill her, he'll become Keziah's servant again, won't he? He will be bound to her, forced to do her bidding." When Tate doesn't answer, I stare at him in horror. "If she has such control over him, why did he go to find her himself? Why not send you?"

"He didn't have a choice." His eyes on mine are grave. "Even before he left, he could already hear Keziah calling him, pulling him to her. That's why he had to go. Even if Antoine wanted to stay, Harper, he couldn't. The pull of her influence is too strong, and she wields it over Antoine without mercy."

"That's what you meant when you asked which way he would choose," I breathe. Tate nods. "And he said he would do what must be done." I remember the bitter tone in his voice. "He meant that if he finds Keziah and Caleb, he will do the same as last time." It isn't a question. I know what he meant. I know it with a cold surety. "He means he will trap himself with them again. Or die. Whatever he has to do to ensure they won't come back."

"It's about more than that. Keziah will be Cass's Maker, too." Tate tilts his chin toward the house. "If Cass transitions, she will be bound to Keziah, just as Antoine is. And Keziah is not one to give up her pets. Caleb has been bound to her for centuries. Keziah will know if Cass transitions. She will come back for her."

We stare at each other in the darkness. "And then it will start all over again. She will have another servant to do her bidding." I finish what he doesn't say. "Is there any way out of it?"

"Antoine told me he would try to find Noya. She is far more knowledgeable than she lets on. She may know a way forward. She may also have the magic to seal the sun in Cass's body. Most of our kind do not carry the sun within them, as Antoine and I do, in totems wrought in our skin. Some have talismans, as Keziah and Caleb do, but they are fragile things, easily weakened, stolen, or lost. Noya may be able to do both—seal the sun within Cass, as well as help her resist Keziah's commands." He looks at me gravely. "But all of that depends upon Antoine being able to resist Keziah's command and choosing to find Noya instead."

"You don't think he can resist her again." I can hear it in his voice, and when he doesn't speak, the dread tugs at my heart again. "You think he will run straight to Keziah and become what he was before. A slave to her worst impulses, a danger to everyone." I meet his eyes. "To me."

"To you, most of all, Harper." Tate's hand rests on my shoulder. "The Antoine I have known for three centuries would have ended Cass tonight without so much as a thought. And before that, he would have killed you, and your brother, it if meant keeping the binding intact. He has done as much and worse over the centuries to ensure that Keziah remained bound and he free of her compulsion. His anger at her power over him has always been the dominant feature of his soul, has nearly always won over my mother's compassion, the medicine woman that lives within him. He has thrown himself into every fight he could find, every war on the face of this earth. He has committed atrocities you would shrink to learn of. Antoine has been utterly ruthless in order to keep the secret of this mansion, and what lies beneath it has tortured his every moment since he became what he is. And yet now, he has risked all of it—for you." Tate shakes his head. "He married you, Harper. Bound himself to you. I still don't understand it, not truly."

"But isn't that a good thing?" I ask tentatively.

"No." The finality in his voice takes me aback. When he meets my eyes, I can see the pain and concern in his. "Even if he does find the strength to resist Keziah's summons and seek Noya out, what do you think will happen to you, Harper? What do you think Keziah will do to you, when she realizes the power you hold over her slave?"

CHAPTER 16

MOONLIGHT

I stand beneath the magnolia tree long after Tate goes back into the kitchen, staring at the blank screen of my phone, wishing that Antoine would call, or text—anything.

Night is growing late. The moon is full and large, high in the sky but already tipping down toward the horizon. Dawn is perhaps four hours away. Not long enough for the decisions that must be made. But could any amount of time truly be enough, I wonder, for such decisions?

"Tessa," I whisper to the night sky. "How did you find the courage to face death, when you knew it was coming for you? What do I say to Cass?"

I try to remember what I said to my twin in those final hours, but I remember only how it felt between us, not what was said. I remember how her hand felt in mine, how every fiber of her being seemed focused on each breath, until finally there was no breath left. I remember the moment I knew she was gone, and that in the end, I wanted her to go, willed her to be at peace.

I know I have never been the same since that day. Tessa's death changed me, as did Mom's. Perhaps, once, I had been a teenager, one half of the Ellory twins, Connor's little sister. But I don't remember ever truly feeling that way. I can't remember a time when I didn't know Tessa was sick, and that perhaps I was the only one who could help her, the only person with a kidney that matched hers. I have no memory at all of my biological father, who died when we were infants. Mom became sick when Tessa and I were barely teenagers ourselves. Despite my telling Antoine earlier tonight that I wanted for just one night to be ordinary, it sometimes seems to me that I wouldn't know what ordinary was even if I found it. In a lifetime of death, there has been little room for ordinary life. And despite all the death I have already seen, here I am again. Standing outside as someone I love dies inside, witness to Cass's suffering, with no more ability to prevent it than I'd been able to prevent Tessa's.

Subconsciously, I touch the scar at my side where my kidney was removed.

"It didn't help her, in the end." I swing around to find Connor silhouetted on the porch behind me, his face shadowed. "Giving Tessa your kidney." His voice is tired and thin as he comes to stand beside me. "Tessa knew she was going to die. She never wanted you to give your kidney to her, to suffer for her. She just didn't know how to tell you that—or how to say goodbye."

"I know that, now." I look at him, guilt coursing through me in sick waves. "I truly am sorry, Connor." I want to touch him, but his face is so stark I don't. "I thought I was doing the right thing in keeping all of this from you. But none of this would have ever happened if I'd just told you the truth. After everything we've been through together . . . I should have known better."

"Yes," says Connor simply. "You should have, Harper." He reaches out and pulls a leaf from the tree, tearing it into pieces that fall unheeded to the ground below. "It's the same for Cass as it was for Tessa," he says roughly. "She knows she's going to die. She's in there with Tate now, talking with him about what will happen. She isn't going to make the transition, Harper." His voice breaks on the words. He swallows hard. "And she doesn't want to wait until dawn."

"But she has to!" I take a step toward the house, panic gripping my throat. "She has to at least wait until we hear from Antoine, or until he comes back . . ." my voice trails off, and I turn away.

"Antoine won't come back, Harper." Connor says it with such certainty that I look at him. "Cass can hear Keziah calling him." His face is dark and closed. "Not clearly, but enough. She can hear Keziah calling *her*." He shakes his head. "She doesn't want that, Harper. She doesn't want to be a weapon that Keziah can use, as Antoine is."

"You don't know that's what he is." I can hear the defensive note in my voice.

"Yes I do, Harper." Connor grasps my arm. "And deep down, so do you. Cass made Tate explain it all. Antoine is gone. If he comes back at all, it will be as a monster, allied to them, to Keziah and Caleb. When tonight is over, there is nothing you and I can do but run from here and hope they don't find us."

"Leave?" I stare at him. "How can you even consider that? How can you even talk about letting Cass die?"

"I can't make her drink, Harper." Despair breaks his voice. "And even if I could, how can I ignore what it means if she does? How do you think Cass could live with herself, knowing that she will likely become the willing slave of a monster—and that her immortality has come at the price of another human life?" He turns back toward the house. "You should go inside and say goodbye to her."

"Connor, wait." I put my hand on his arm and steel myself for what I need to say. "What if Cass took my life?"

"What?" My brother stares at me blankly.

I don't know what I'm about to say until the words come

out. "I would gladly have given my life for Tessa's." My words seem torn from somewhere deep inside me. "No matter what I said, I knew that Tessa didn't want my kidney. But I didn't truly want to live without her, either. My choice wasn't entirely selfless, Connor. Part of me hoped I'd never wake up from that operation. That both of us wouldn't." I look at him, letting him see the pain I always keep hidden, the pain we both know we hide from each other, in silence and house plans and paintings on a wall. "Even when we came here, it felt like barely half a life, one I could see little point in living. It was only when I met Antoine . . ." I swallow painfully. "But now he's gone," I say softly. "And, as you say, he isn't coming back. But it doesn't have to be the same for Cass and you."

"I'm not even having this discussion with you." Connor's face is closed and grim. "How could you suggest it, after all we've lost? Perhaps you didn't care about your life back then. But I did, Harper. I do. Do you truly think I'd accept your life for Cass's?"

"It's my fault, Connor. All of this is my fault." My hand tightens on his arm. "But you still have a chance for happiness."

"And you don't?" Connor pulls away from me. The moonlight turns his eyes to dark pools that are no longer angry, just tired and resigned. "Do you think I came to Deepwater simply because I wanted to restore this mansion? I came here because I was terrified that if we stayed one more day in Baton Rouge, surrounded by memories, that I'd lose you to them. You were fading before my eyes, Harper. You barely ate. You talked in your sleep." He takes a ragged breath. "You spoke to Tessa every night, crying for her, telling her you would come home to her soon. It got so I was afraid to sleep, in case I woke up to find you were gone, too." He puts his hands on my shoulders. "You're the only family I have left. You and I, Tessa—we all had to grow up too young." He pauses. "I'm not going to pretend I'm not angry that you married Antoine, or that I understand why you couldn't tell me. But I do know that you've been through more than most people endure in a lifetime. If anyone deserves a chance at happiness, it's you." He stops again, and when he resumes speaking, his voice is rough and uneven. "Whether I understand it or not, part of me knows it was Antoine, and whatever it is between you, that brought you back to life. But that doesn't mean that without him you have nothing left to live for. And it certainly doesn't mean I will allow you let go of the life we have, simply because Antoine is gone."

"And I can't let Cass give up hers." Tears clutch my throat. "We can't let her die, Connor. I won't."

He shakes his head. "I can't make her drink, Harper."

"None of you can." We turn, startled, to find Cass standing behind us, flanked by Tate and Avery. Her face is set and frightened, but I can see the resolution in it. "Tate has explained to me what happens, if I drain someone to complete the transition. And also what happens between vampire and Maker. I will become someone else, someone new. I may not even have control over my own actions." She meets my eyes. "I won't be myself anymore. I don't want this. Any of it."

"But you can't just die." Avery grips Cass's arms. "Please, Cass."

"It's my decision," says Cass simply. "And I need you all to respect it." Her eyes slide to Connor, and I see the pleading in them. My brother's mouth tightens into a rictus smile that is as unconvincing as his voice is when he says: "I understand."

He doesn't. I know he doesn't. And even if Connor says he won't let me die, I can't truly believe he is ready to let Cass go.

I stare after them as they walk slowly back toward the house, my heart twisting. Connor is simply someone who has seen so much death, he no longer knows how to fight for life. Perhaps he is right, and I am just the same.

All I know is that after all we've been through, after losing so much, I can't bear the thought of losing Cass as well. Even if

Antoine is gone—and I can't truly believe he is—surely there has to be a way to save Cass.

There are four hours until dawn.

My hand tightens on the Moonvine that winds up the columns on the porch, feeling the cool petals, delicate yet strong under my hand as they open to the night. "There has to be another way," I whisper to Tessa. "Please help me find it."

CHAPTER 17

MAGIC

*M*y phone lights up just as I am about to walk inside. My finger shakes as I push the button to take the call. "Hello? Noya?"

"Harper." Tension crackles down the phone in Noya's voice. "I was in a motel near Natchez today, getting some rest before the drive. I had my phone turned off, which is why I missed your calls." I start to speak but she cuts me off. "Before I went to the motel, I was leaving Deepwater, driving on the highway north, when I stopped at a little church I remember on the way."

I feel a shiver on my skin, remember the emerald sliding onto my finger. *I, Harper Ellory, take you, Antoine . . .* "I know the place," I say softly.

"When I went inside," Noya continues, "I could feel something on the air. A chill. And it smelled like burning, the same as it did when I was in the cellar." She hesitates. "Harper—is it possible that the seal has been opened again?"

"Not just possible." I take a deep breath. "Avery opened the cellar by accident, Noya. Keziah and Caleb escaped. And it gets worse." I'm about to rush into the details when she cuts me off again.

"I thought so." There is something tired in her voice that stops me. "I could barely keep my eyes open when I left that church. I pulled into first motel I found. I think I knew even then that something was trying to keep me here. I just didn't want to know. I guess that's why I turned my phone off."

"Noya." I try not to sound too eager. "You haven't talked to Antoine, have you?"

There is a long pause before she answers. "No, Harper." I can hear her sympathy, and it hurts. "I got a message from him, then from Tate, and you. I tried to call him back. But he isn't answering."

"If he hasn't come to find you," I say dully, "Antoine isn't coming back."

I swallow hard and explain, as quickly as I can, what has happened. "Cass is determined to die, Noya. I don't know how to change her mind." On the other end of the line, I hear an odd sound, like rushing wind. "Noya?" I cover my other ear, trying to concentrate on the bad line. "Can you hear me?"

When Noya speaks again, her voice is trembling slightly. "Tell Cass to hold on until I get there. I have an idea of what we can do. I'm on my way."

Feeling the first surge of hope since seeing Cass's body on the floor, I rush into the house to find Avery and Tate in the kitchen. "They're upstairs," Tate answers my unspoken question. "They wanted some privacy to say goodbye." I take the stairs two at a time, feeling the old wood soft beneath my feet, and push Connor's door open. "Noya called!" Cass doesn't look up from the protective circle of Connor's arms. "She's coming. She's barely an hour from here."

It's Connor who answers. "Cass is growing weaker, Harper."

"Tate says that if I hold on until dawn without drinking, the first rays of sun will kill me." Cass's voice is thin and thready and she doesn't look at me when she speaks. "But he can burn me before then. Before the cravings become—unbearable."

"It's becoming harder for her to be near people." Connor strokes the head against his chest, and I know there's no point in telling him it's dangerous for him to be holding her. "She won't hurt me," he says quietly, reading my thoughts.

"Please, Cass," I plead. "Hold on. Just for a little longer."

If I close my eyes, I am back in the hospital, holding Tessa's hand. *Hold on, Tessa. Just for a little longer.* Connor meets my eyes and I know he is remembering, too, the prayers both silent and spoken we made, day after day, and the dull finality when we realized none of them had been heard.

Cass raises her head. "Is Antoine with Noya?" I try not to recoil at the fierce red in her eyes. It's as if the blood thirst is creeping into every cell of her body.

I shake my head, unable to find my voice to answer her.

"I'm sorry, Harper." Despite the bloodthirst and all the reasons Cass has to hate me, I can hear only compassion in her voice. "I hoped he would resist. I thought, for a moment, that I could feel him trying."

"Can you?" I ask before I can stop myself, then feel utterly ashamed that I would even think to ask such a thing, in such a moment. "I'm sorry," I mumble, turning for the door. "I shouldn't have asked."

"Yes, I can feel him." Cass's voice is weak, but clear, and it stops me in my tracks. "And also no. I can sense him, but only as a feeling, like a shadow on the edges of my mind. Keziah, though—Harper, she's angry. So angry. She wants Antoine. And me, too. She's calling us both to join her."

I frown. "Then Antoine isn't already with her?"

Cass shakes her head slowly. "I don't think so. If he was, she wouldn't be so angry. So determined to come for me." Her red eyes glow, and I realize it's with fear. "That's why I have to end this." She looks between Connor and me. "Keziah knows I haven't transitioned, and she isn't happy. I can't still be here when she comes for me. I have to be dead—or I will become hers. I can feel it, feel *her*, inside me."

She shudders, huddling into Connor, who looks at me with eyes so filled with pain I can't bear it. "Just a little longer," I mouth, in the silent way we mastered when we had to speak over first Mom's dying body, then Tessa's. "Until Noya gets here."

He gives me a tiny nod, and I back out of the room. I'm terrified that I will return to find Cass gone. I remember all the nights in the hospital when I was afraid to leave Tessa's side even to visit the bathroom, so scared she would die without her hand in mine. Eventually the nurses stopped asking if I needed a drink or a chair and just left Connor and me there, sitting on either side of the bed, holding a hand each, trying to breathe a last moment of life into our beautiful sister.

Now Connor is having to do that again and I know, no matter what he says, that a piece of him is dying with every breath of life that is leaving Cass's body. My brother doesn't deserve this. He came to Deepwater to give us a new life. Instead, we have found more death, more people we love that are being taken from us.

Antoine's face floats before my eyes, his scent somehow lingering in the air around me. I remember his words at the beginning of the party tonight: *And what happens at the end of the night?* I hear his voice as if he were right next to me, and I fight hot tears.

You leave, I answer him fiercely in my mind. *I lose you all over again. My brother loses Cass. And we're all alone, just as we were before any of this began.*

I go into my bedroom, unable to face Connor's gaunt face. On the ground below, the remains of the party are scattered down the slope toward the river, red plastic cups like a trail leading toward the dock. I look at the place where the men from the bayou laid only hours earlier. It seems a lifetime ago. I frown, remembering the odd exchange I heard before Keziah and Caleb escaped, and go downstairs.

"Tate." He's sitting quietly in the kitchen with Jeremiah and Avery, and they all look up when I come in. "The men who were here earlier, from the bayou. They knew about this place. What did Antoine mean when he said they should have stayed on their side of the river?"

Tate glances at Avery, then back at me. I can tell he is reluctant to speak.

"They have Natchez blood." It is Avery who speaks, her voice soft and tired. "Keziah told me that when she told me where to find them. I invited them because she told me to."

"Why?"

"To drink from them." Tate's voice is curt. "Keziah is seeking the most power she can find. When she drained Cass, she absorbed almost the entire life force of the living descendant of Samuel, the magician who wove the spell that kept her bound. She had already drunk from Avery, who is descended from the medicine woman who wove the Natchez magic. The men from the bayou are something else, descended from a different tribe, with different magic."

"What kind of magic?" I look between them. "What are those men?"

Avery glances at Tate. "I only know the stories Cass's mom told me. Old stories. I didn't think any of them were true."

My mouth twists. "After everything we've seen, do you really doubt any of those stories?"

"They're true," says Tate. "Or they were, once. The tribe from the bayou were shapeshifters, rumored to be able to take on the form of any animal they chose." His face tightens momentarily. "They were not exactly my family's enemies, nor were they entirely allies. They also guarded their magic jealously. I thought there were none left living. Certainly none left with that kind of magic in their veins. Until tonight."

"Are they still shapeshifters?" I ask, my tongue stumbling over the word. It seems ridiculous to even be saying it aloud.

"I don't know," Tate says frankly. "But maybe Antoine does. It was only when I saw them together tonight, heard the odd questions they asked, that I realized what they were. I'm not sure if they even know themselves. Perhaps they know only the stories, too." He smiles at Jeremiah and Avery as if he's finished speaking, then subtly tilts his head toward the corridor. I follow him out of the room to a discreet distance as Jeremiah and Avery start talking again.

His eyes are serious when they meet mine. "I do know one thing: Keziah knew exactly what they were." His low voice is meant only for my ears. "Whether she saw them in Avery's mind or simply knew somehow, I don't know, but she told Avery how to find the bayou Natchez. Keziah wanted their blood and whatever power lives in it. And now she has it. She and Caleb drained them all, nearly to death. It was only Antoine's blood that saved their lives."

"Antoine fed them his blood?" I stare at Tate, aghast.

"They would have died if he had not, Harper."

And now Antoine himself could die, I think but don't say. Fear claws at me. He needed every ounce of strength to resist Keziah. Instead, he used it to save the lives of creatures we don't even understand and who could just as easily prove to be enemies as friends.

I feel angry and frustrated and above all, sad.

I glance at the clock. An hour has passed, and still Noya is not here.

I sit down beside Tate, and together we wait.

Less than three hours remain before dawn.

CHAPTER 18

MAKER

*A*lmost another hour passes before we hear stumbling footsteps on the stairs. We leap to our feet as one when Cass enters the kitchen, leaning weakly on Connor. She looks terrible. Her skin is chalky, her lips pale and dry. But it is her eyes that are truly terrifying. There is barely any pupil left, just a blank sheen of dull red with a faint pinprick of black in the center. She keeps her head down and leans against the wall, at a distance from us.

"Noya isn't coming." Connor's voice is rough. "She should have been here by now. If she isn't, something's happened."

"I can't feel Antoine anymore," Cass rasps weakly. "I can only hear Keziah summoning me. Her voice is getting stronger. She's coming, and when she gets here, I won't be able to fight her." She looks briefly at Tate and then away. "I can't wait any longer."

"You have until dawn," Tate says. "You don't have to do this yet, Cass. If Keziah does come, I will see to it you don't fall into her power."

"You can't," says Cass despairingly. "You don't understand the hold she has over me." The red eyes pass over me then turn away. "Antoine is lost. Nobody could resist a force like Keziah's. I can feel it, pulling me, like every cell of my body wants to go to her. If I wasn't so weak, I'd be gone already."

I turn to Tate. "There must be a way to resist it. You're able to separate from Antoine—"

"Separate." Tate cuts me off harshly. "Not resist."

"Then tell her how to separate from Keziah."

"You aren't hearing me, Harper." Tate pushes back restlessly from the table. "I can separate from Antoine because I don't have to resist him. He has never wanted me at his side, not since the day I transitioned. He has never summoned or commanded me. But even without him calling me, still the bond drew me close. For a time, it nearly drove me insane."

"Why?" Avery asks. "How was it hard, if Antoine never commanded you?"

Tate meets her eyes. "To be controlled by one's Maker is hard. But to feel the power of that bond and to be ignored by them—believe me, that is just as painful. Especially when there is no way to stop loving the Maker to whom you are bound."

Avery's eyes flicker between Connor and Cass, who thankfully don't notice. She sees me looking at her and reddens, looking down at the table. I know she's wondering if Cass's change will mean the end for Cass and Connor, regardless of what will happen.

"Antoine was as my brother." Tate goes on, pretending not to notice Avery's embarrassment. "Three centuries later, he still is. But in all that time, never once has he called for me. Whenever I have sought him out, he has run without looking back." He meets my eyes. "These past days are as much time as we have spent in each other's company in many years, and asking me to take care of you, Harper, is the first request he has ever made of me."

I sense he is trying to tell me something beyond the story of his bond with Antoine, but the awareness happens on the periphery of my mind. All I can consciously think of is Cass. Her eyes glow dully as Tate speaks, and when he finishes she pushes herself away from the wall.

"Well, I won't be a slave to that bond." Her voice is stronger than before. "I want to end this, Tate. I won't discuss it any more. You said it was my decision, and now I'm making it." She glances around at us, and when we all look away from the fierce red gaze, her mouth tightens in a hard, hurt line that bears no resemblance to the gentle girl I've known since I arrived. "You know what I'm becoming," she says in a low voice. "I can feel it like a savage animal inside me. When I look at you, all I see is the blood beneath your skin. All I can think of is killing you." She looks back at Tate. "Please," she says simply.

Tate's eyes flicker to Connor. "It has to be her choice."

Connor doesn't speak. He tries to reach for Cass's hand, but she leaps away with that same disturbing swiftness, cowering against the doorframe leading to the porch. "Don't," she rasps. "You're not safe with me anymore, Connor." Her head whips around and she becomes very still. "There's a car." Her body quivers with tension.

Tate is already through the door and on the porch. "Antoine's in that car," he murmurs. "I can feel him." As the first glimmer of headlights break through the trees, he looks at me, an odd expression on his face. I remember his words of a moment ago: "Whenever I have sought him out, he has run without looking back . . . asking me to take care of you, Harper, is the first request he has ever made of me."

But he hasn't run. Not this time. That is what Tate was trying to tell me. This time, he has taken up the Maker's bond. Commanded Tate to stay, to take care of me.

And he has come back.

I stare at the headlights bobbing along the road, unable to speak, or even to fathom what Antoine's return might mean.

"It's Noya's car," says Tate as the vehicle turns through the gate. "And she's with him."

"It isn't Keziah," breathes Cass.

"No." Tate is looking at her and frowning. "Can you hold on just a little longer, Cass?" His eyes flicker to the horizon. It's still dark, but the night has become deathly still with the silence of early hours, and the quality of light is changing, entering that darkest phase before the first hint of dawn.

Cass looks at him and I can feel the desperation warring with hope inside her. "Not for long," she whispers. "It hurts, Tate."

"I know." Tate is at Cass's side, with an arm around her, shooting Connor a warning glance as my brother reaches for her. "You have to keep your distance now," he says to Connor, but his words are for all of us. "It's too hard for her to be close to blood." Connor steps back, grim faced.

Noya's rental is moving fast, and before it has even stopped, the doors are opening, Noya coming out of the passenger seat and Antoine out of the driver's. There is no pretense of humanity in the speed with which he reaches the porch. I've barely registered his presence before he and Tate have Cass with them in the shadows of the red magnolia, heads bent together. I can see only Antoine's back, tall and hard and as closed to me as he's ever been.

Whatever is going to happen here, he will not have me be a part of it.

CHAPTER 19

DAWN

"We need to leave immediately." Tate's face is grave. Antoine is bundling Cass into the rental, Noya already starting the engine. "There's a Natchez site close by," Tate says. "An old place of power. It's the best place to work the sun magic."

"Does that mean you've found a way to save her?" Connor is already pushing past me, running for the car.

"Connor—" Tate grasps his arm, but when he sees Connor's face, white and set, he lets him go again. Connor yanks open the door and I hear Antoine's curt voice, though I can't make out what he says. Then Connor is inside, and the car is spinning gravel, heading back down the driveway. I'm already making for my Mustang.

"You should stay here, Harper." I glare at Tate and start the engine. Avery and Jeremiah are already piling into Avery's car. Tate shakes his head and gets in beside me. "I'll give you directions," he says resignedly.

The Natchez site is barely ten miles away. "How are they going to save her?" I ask. The light is growing with alarming swiftness. I've never noticed before how fast dawn comes. The delicate scent of moonflower hangs in the damp air, clinging to my face as I drive.

When Tate doesn't answer immediately, I glance at him. "How, Tate?"

He clicks his tongue and looks away. "Noya." He doesn't meet my eyes.

"She's working the magic?"

"No."

It takes a moment for his meaning to sink in. "Noya's the sacrifice," I whisper. My hands on the steering wheel feel numb. I'm grateful the road is empty. I'm not really aware of driving, or of anything around me. "We can't let her do that."

"It's her choice." Tate's voice is quiet. "Noya has Huntington's disease, Harper. It's a nerve condition. There isn't a cure." He looks at me. "Noya's been feeling the effects for a while now. She knows what comes next—a slow, painful death, over which she will have no control. She chose this instead."

We drive in silence for a while, and I think back to Noya's exhaustion, the tired way she had struggled to go down the stairs to the cellar door. "Even so," I say eventually, "Cass will never agree."

"Do you honestly think Connor will let her say no?"

I don't answer that. I know he's right. Tate points to a sign, and I turn down a side road lined with tall trees. Ahead of us, the road opens into a parking garage in front of a tourist shop, all deserted so early in the morning. The rental is pulled up at a careless angle. Noya, Antoine, Cass, and Connor are walking across the ground toward a mound of raised earth. By the time we park and follow them, the last stars are disappearing and the horizon is threaded with gold.

"If Noya is the sacrifice," I say, "who will work the sun magic?"

Tate nods at Antoine's tall figure, striding toward the mound of earth, carrying Cass in his arms, Connor on one side and

Noya on the other. "Antoine?" I stare at Tate in confusion. "How?"

"You forget," says Tate quietly. "Antoine was made with my mother's blood. Atsila was the wisest medicine woman known to our people. She lives within him still. Antoine may not be able to work the magic of the living, but this, the magic of sun and of vampires, is in his power." He glances at me. "It's Atsila he will call on now. I should know. It was Antoine who bound the sun into my body."

I don't have time to ponder this revelation. Ahead of us Antoine is climbing the mound, lowering Cass gently to the ground, holding out a hand, warning Connor to stay away. In the growing light, Noya's face is pale and resolute.

It's all happening too fast.

I break into a run, stumbling over the ground. "Cass!" I call, my voice cracking. "Wait!" I reach Connor's side, and my brother's hand grasps my arm in a vise-strong grip.

"No," he says, his voice uneven. His face is stark white, his eyes flat and drained. "Don't interfere, Harper." I look up to find Antoine's eyes on me. They are the deep stormy sea again, tumbled with emotions I can't read, an internal battle he is fighting alone. He shakes his head, a slight movement, but as final as if there was a wall around him. His eyes slide to Tate at my side. "Keep them safe," he says. "They're coming."

"Keziah and Caleb?" I swing around to face Tate. "They're coming here?" I look at Antoine again, seeing the tension in the hard lines of his body, the carved trenches in his face, and suddenly I understand the war I can see in his eyes. "She's calling you, isn't she?" My heart twists. "Keziah is summoning you."

"She's calling them both," says Connor harshly. "And it's taking every ounce of willpower he's got to resist." His eyes don't move from Cass. "Cass can't fight at all anymore. She's—" his voice breaks. "She's losing her mind, Harper."

"Is that normal?" It's Jeremiah, his arm around a frightened-looking Avery. He addresses his question to Tate.

"No," says Tate shortly. "It's not normal. It's not good, either. They need to hurry." He looks at us. "Stay here." He climbs the mound and speaks to Noya, clasping her in a brief embrace, then his hand rests on Antoine's shoulder. I can't hear him, but I see his lips move: *Now.*

Then he is at our side again. "Whatever you do," he grips Connor's shoulders, "none of you move. Don't interfere and don't leave this place. Do you understand?" He stares at us until we nod, but none of us need his instruction. I don't think we could move even if we wanted to. Our eyes are locked on the tableau on the earth mound, where the three figures are silhouetted in the growing dawn. As we watch, Antoine kneels down, leaning over Cass's body which is unnaturally, terribly still.

"Where are you going?" Avery asks Tate.

"To the entrance. To stand guard."

He doesn't need to say against what. We all know what's coming for us. Tate is gone with his own words, disappearing into the pale predawn.

"Look," Jeremiah mutters at my side. He nods his head to the east, where the faint gold thread is shimmering into a band.

On the mound, Antoine turns to face the horizon.

It is beginning.

CHAPTER 20

MADE

*A*ntoine's arms come up high over his head. Cass's prone figure arches on the ground. He lowers his hands, the flat palms seeming to soothe Cass's tortured body, turning her until she lies face down, with Antoine standing over her.

It's then I see the blade he holds, gleaming in the first rays of the coming day.

"What is he doing?" Connor surges forward, and now it's me who must restrain him.

"He's giving her the sun." I flinch as the blade sears through the air and plunges into Cass's flesh, directly into the base of her spine. Cass screams, an agonising, heart rending sound. "He's sealing the sun inside her."

"He's killing her!" Connor lunges against me, and Jeremiah grasps his other arm, helping me hold him.

"Connor!" I force him to look at me. "Antoine is saving Cass from the only thing that can kill her now. He's the only one who can do this. Leave him be."

On the mound, Cass is still screaming, bucking against the knife in her flesh. Antoine holds it there, unflinching, his other hand holding her down, his lips moving as he speaks words I

138

can't hear. The rising sun makes a halo around him, and he seems to shimmer in the dawn, the light falling onto him and into him as if he is a lightning rod, traveling down to the knife in his hand, making it gleam.

He calls a sharp command. Noya drops to her knees. Despite the knife Antoine holds still gleaming in her back, Cass's arms come up, pulling the slender woman to her with savage triumph. The sound of her teeth tearing through flesh is raw and terrifying in the silent dawn. Noya gives a short, sharp cry, and Connor flinches beside me. Antoine stands immobile above them. I can see only the deep rise and fall of his chest, the tension in his clenched fist on the knife, as Cass drinks, on and on. The way she takes Noya's body is almost carnal, the embrace of a lover. It feels almost indecent to watch it, but none of us can look away.

Finally Antoine releases the knife, and he steps back, his body oddly slumped. Cass's head comes back, her blood-covered mouth bared in an animal snarl. She wipes her mouth with one hand and drops Noya's body as carelessly as if it were discarded rubbish. The movement is callous, shocking, and utterly different to the Cass I've known since I came to Deepwater.

Cass pushes Noya's limp body away from her. I can see her in profile only, but already Cass seems different, as if her body is lengthening before my eyes, her human limbs smoothing out into something both harder and somehow more malleable. She folds over at an impossible angle then springs apart like a trap released, a primal scream ripping from her throat and cutting the air. Antoine steps forward and reaches for the knife in her back. It comes away blazing white, like metal right out of the forge. He replaces the blade with his hands, holding them on the base of her spine, and Cass's body jolts again.

From Noya's fallen corpse, a strange mist, like pearlescent smoke, spirals into the air, weaving around Antoine and Cass's joined bodies. It wraps tighter around them in an intricate pattern, moving faster and faster, until their forms are almost hidden from view, enclosed in a shimmering web that gleams in the first rays of the brilliant sun. Antoine's voice rises with the sun, chanting words in a language I don't understand, and I seem to hear Noya's voice entwined with his, the two harmonizing in a sound that grows in power and volume, feeding the web around them, until the mound is a pulsing ball of light and sound.

As it reaches a crescendo, the sun bursts into full life over the horizon, and the day is born. The web splinters into a million diamond shards of light that temporarily blind us. In the moment before it disappears, the brilliant shards seem to wrap around me, enclosing me in a glittering shroud in which I hear Noya's voice. It is around me, inside me, her words meant, I know, for my ears alone.

"He has sworn to protect you all." I know without explanation that she means Antoine. "It was the price of my sacrifice. Make sure he keeps that promise." Then her voice is gone, the shards of light disappearing into the daylight, leaving only the mundane sounds of day around us. Noya's corpse is slack on the mound. Cass's body is still beside it. Antoine stands above her, chest heaving, knife still in his hand.

Slowly, Cass raises her head, then her torso, staring at Antoine. He is facing me, but his eyes are on Cass. I've never seen him look so exhausted, his face craggy and lined as granite. But it's his eyes that make my heart lurch in fear. They are dark, empty pits, as if all hope has left him.

Cass turns to face us, but it is no longer Cass whose perfect mouth curves in a slow, knowing smile. Beside me, Connor sucks in his breath. Cass's blazing crimson eyes rest briefly on him and her smile deepens, becomes yet more seductive. Then she stills, like an animal sensing danger, and her eyes move past him, coming to rest on me. Something dark and dangerous stirs in their depths and a low, chilling growl rises from her chest. Perfectly white, even teeth scrape her lower lip hungrily.

I want to reach out to her, try to calm her, but something warns me that any move I make will mean death. I stand still as the dawn, holding those crimson eyes with all the love and courage I can muster.

"Cass," says Antoine hoarsely. He takes a step toward her, but he sways on his feet, and I realize in horror that he barely has the strength to stand. "Don't touch her." His voice is still commanding despite its gravelly edge. If you hurt Harper, I will kill you myself, I swear it."

Cass pauses and turns disdainful eyes to him. "You don't have the strength to even try," she says scornfully, and I hear Connor's shocked intake of breath.

She takes the first step toward me and despite knowing that this is Cass, the beautiful, gentle girl who's the closest thing to a best friend that I have, I take an instinctive step backward, my hand closing on Connor's arm. Cass's eyes slide to me. "She wants you." She smiles coldly. "Keziah wants you, Harper."

Then her head snaps up and she freezes, as if every nerve ending is alert. Antoine is at her side in an instant. "Don't." His hand grips her arm. "You can fight her, Cass. Noya's spirit is inside you. Use her to help you resist. Fight it, Cass!"

The perfect face whips around to stare at him. Cass looks down at where his hand holds her arm, then back at him. "Why?" she says simply.

With a simple twist of her arm she is free, and then she is right in front of me, her skin gleaming like polished teak, the unsettling eyes looking at me with detached curiosity. One long finger reaches out and strokes my face wonderingly, as if feeling skin for the first time. Her touch is insidious, like something is trying to slide under the surface. "Keziah says: *Soon, Harper. But not yet.*" She bares her teeth in a smile so chilling it makes me recoil. "Not yet."

And then she is gone, so fast it's as if she was never here, and Connor is roaring at Antoine to do something, to go after her.

But Antoine is staring at me, his eyes cavernous, dark holes. He says my name, once: "Harper."

Then he topples to the ground beside Noya's dead body, his figure as still as her corpse.

"Antoine!" I race up the mound of earth, my face tingling strangely where Cass touched it. I fall to the ground beside his prone body, trying not to look at Noya's lifeless form, at her sightless eyes staring up at the sky. I'm vaguely aware of Connor roaring Cass's name, running in the direction she fled, but I can't think of anything but the man lying facedown before me. I try to roll him over, my breath sobbing in my throat, but he's so big it takes all my strength. When finally I move him, his eyes are closed, and he's barely breathing. I take the knife from his hand and cut my own, opening a crimson line across it. I barely feel the touch of the blade. I hold it to his mouth. "Drink." I push my hand at the still lips. "Drink!"

"Harper!" Avery is staring at me in horror. "What are you doing?"

"Get Tate." My voice cracks. "Go, Avery. Please." Jeremiah kneels opposite me, his eyes wide. "Why isn't he drinking?" I turn my hand this way and that. "He should be drinking, Jeremiah." He doesn't answer me, just stares fearfully at Antoine's still figure. "Tate!" I call, crying between breaths.

Then I'm pushed aside, and Tate is there, bending over Antoine's body. His face is grave. "He won't drink," I stammer, picking up the knife again. "Maybe if I make the cut bigger—"

"If it was blood that he needed, he would drink." Tate is staring at Antoine, a faint crease between his brows.

"Then what is it?"

He looks up at me, his eyes dark and hollow. "I don't know."

"What do you mean, you don't know?" I push him aside and press my hand to Antoine's lips again. "Please," I whisper.

"Please wake up. Please don't leave me. Not now. Not like this." I can't stop talking, saying his name, and when he doesn't respond, I lie down beside him, pressing my whole body against his, feeling the lean, hard length of him against me, still so strong and solid I can't believe he could possibly be gone. I press my head against his heart, horrified at the faint, irregular beat.

"Do something," I plead, my hands curling inside his shirt, one on his heart and the other feeling the place where the totem marks his spine, just as it now does Cass's.

Cass. Maybe that's it, I think. I find Tate's eyes, watching us both worriedly. "Is it because of the magic he gave to Cass? When he did it, did he lose his own? Is that it? Is that what's wrong with him?"

Tate shakes his head slowly. "I don't think so, Harper. I think it exhausted him, yes. And he was already tired, after—" He glances at Avery, and his voice breaks off.

"After what?" Jeremiah looks between us.

"After he fed the bayou boys at the party his blood." I'm too upset to care about protecting Avery's feelings. "They were attacked by Keziah, almost drained to death. Antoine gave them his blood to save their lives, but he lost a lot of his strength doing it." Avery looks away, biting her lip.

"Why would he do that?" Jeremiah's face is tight and angry. "Why would he make himself weak when he knew he'd have to face Keziah? How could he do that?"

"He couldn't just let them die, Jeremiah." Tate's voice is harsh with worry. "But even that wouldn't do this to him." He shakes his head. "I've never seen anything like this before."

"Stop talking!" I press myself closer to the still body, inhaling the cedar and sunlight scent of him, the scent of happiness and a day in a church when I dared to believe he might hold me forever. "You can't be gone," I whisper against his face. "You promised me, Antoine." I pick up his hand, so large and sure, and touch the wedding band on his ring finger, holding it against the emerald on my own. "Always, remember? You promised me. *Always.*"

"Harper!" I look up to find Tate watching me, an odd look in his eyes. It's Avery who spoke, however, and when she says my name again—"Harper"—there is a strange tone to her voice that makes us all turn. "Look." She points to the ground below us.

Two of the bayou men are standing there, looking up at us, their faces closed and cautious. One is Remy, the man who had seemed to be their leader at the party. The other is the man Tate had restrained, the one who had stared at my emerald ring. They wear only threadbare denim shorts, their torsos covered in dirt.

In between them, reaching as high as their waists, staring at us with golden eyes that gleam with a preternatural light, is a huge, red wolf.

Tate leaps to his feet and stands in front of us, slightly bent at the waist, a low snarl in the back of his throat. The wolf goes very still and bares its teeth, growling softly. Remy puts a restraining hand on its head.

The hand that isn't touching the wolf comes up in a placating gesture. "We don't want any trouble." Remy eyes Tate warily. "We came to help." He nods at Antoine. "We know what's wrong with your friend." Tate is still bent in a defensive position, staring at the wolf.

"What do you know?" I don't care how dangerous the animal looks or why it's here. "What's wrong with him? Can you fix it?"

"Harper." Tate shakes his head warningly.

Ignoring him, I stand up, still holding Antoine's hand between my own. "Tell me."

"Look at his other arm." Remy nods at Antoine's arm on the opposite side from me. "The one he fed us with." I scramble around Antoine's still figure and pull his arm up. "Turn it over," Remy says, "and roll his sleeve up." I do and gasp in horror at the ugly wound marring the bronze skin.

"What is it?" The wound is ragged at the edges and black inside, just as Antoine's eyes had been when he collapsed after the sun magic. The flesh inside it looks empty and dead, like a cave, as if the blackness is tunneling inside him.

"It's because he fed us." The man on the other side of the wolf makes a noise of protest, and Remy glares at him. "Leave be, Will. We'd all be dead if it wasn't for him."

"And now you're going to give them the secrets they need to finish the job." The man called Will spits to one side, eyeing us suspiciously. "This is a dumb idea, Remy."

"And it ain't your place to argue it." Remy glares at him then turns back to us. "Our people haven't become wolf for centuries. We thought it was nothing more than old stories. Until last night." He nods at Antoine. "Until he fed us. Then this happened." He nods at the wolf at his side. "And not just to my brother, here. By the time we all got to our side of the river last night, every one of us had become wolf." He shakes his head, as if still marveling at it. "Every single one." Seeing the impatience on my face, he goes on quickly. "Unfortunately my brother Henri shifted to wolf before your man had finished feeding the rest of us." He shrugs apologetically. "It seems that in wolf form, we don't have the same control we do as men. Henri bit him." He nods at the wound on Antoine's arm. "None of us know much of the old stories," Remy goes on. "But we do know that our bites are fatal to—your kind." He glances at Tate. "The only cure is blood from the wolf that bit you, while it's still in wolf form." The man named Will makes a noise of disgust and spits again. Remy rounds on him. "That thing that escaped last night drained us all of blood, Will. You'd be dead now, if it weren't for him. We'd all be. Instead we're alive, and we have our magic inside us again." He nods at Antoine. "Because he fed us."

He turns back to Tate. "We may have been enemies in the past," he says quietly. "But we all owe that man our lives. We tracked you to here to offer you our help."

"Then help him." I ignore Tate's warning frown. "Please. Before it's too late."

"Harper—" Jeremiah starts, but he stops when he sees my face.

Tate comes close to my side. "Wolves have murdered more of our kind than anything else," he murmurs in my ear. "They're dangerous and unpredictable. We can't trust them."

"And if we don't, Antoine is dead." I look at Remy. "Do what you have to. And if you get in the way," I stare grimly at Tate, "I'll ask them if that wolf is still hungry for vampire blood."

Remy's mouth twitches. "Seems like it's you they should fear, not us," he says, grinning at me as he walks up. He kneels at Antoine's side. "Come on over here, Henri." He coaxes the wolf forward with one hand. It whimpers, then growls, digging its claws into the earth, shuddering the closer it gets to Antoine's body. Remy shrugs at me apologetically. "It goes against our instincts." He nods at the knife in my hand. "Give me that. I'll need to cut to get the blood."

Tate tenses. I glare at him and hand Remy the knife. Swiftly, he cuts the wolf at the shoulder, a thin red line that beads immediately. "Lift his body," I instruct Tate and Jeremiah. "And you," I say to Remy, "hold your brother still."

He grins at me. "Yes, ma'am."

I carefully cradle Antoine's head, bringing it against the wolf's shoulder. The animal shudders and cries, trying to shrink from the lips pressed to its side, but the two men hold it still, even if Will is swearing continuously under his breath as he does so.

"Drink, Antoine," I murmur, fear and hope clawing at my heart in equal measure. "Please drink."

For a moment nothing happens, and I feel dread yawn before me like the dark wound on his arm. Then: "Look!" Avery points at Antoine's arm.

"It's closing," I breathe. "It's working." I look up and Remy gives me the ghost of a wink. "Our secret," he says. "Can't have everyone knowing."

Antoine's eyes open, then flare in alarm. With a roar, he flings the wolf away from him and leaps to his feet, shaking off the arms holding him and looking around wildly.

"Well," Remy says dryly. "I think we can safely say he's back."

CHAPTER 21

ALWAYS

he bayou men leave soon after Antoine's recovery.

"The one that drained us," Remy addresses Antoine as he turns to go, "we tracked her and her two friends to the river. They've crossed it, gone onto our lands."

Antoine's eyes narrow slightly. "What will you do?"

"Kill them," Will answers promptly. "If we find them." I'm glad Connor isn't here. Not even men who turn into wolves, I suspect, would be safe if he heard them threaten Cass.

"Perhaps you might take a little advice," says Antoine with a slight smile, "from someone who has known that particular demon for a long time. Stay away from her and her two companions. She has bested creatures far more dangerous than you will ever be."

"We'll take it under consideration." But by the gleam in Remy's eye and the way his hand tightens on the growling wolf at his side, I suspect he feels Antoine is vastly underestimating the wolves' capabilities.

"You know they won't listen," murmurs Tate as we watch them slip into the trees across the clearing.

"Then they will die," Antoine says flatly. He looks around. "Where's your brother?"

"He ran after Cass."

Antoine frowns. "They will already be long gone. He won't find them."

"I doubt that will stop him looking."

Antoine shakes his head and gives me a wry smile. "Stubbornness is a family trait, it seems." His eyes fall on Noya's lifeless body, and his smile fades. "Jeremiah, why don't you take Harper and Avery and look for Connor? Tate and I will—take care of things here."

Tate glances sideways at me. "I'll take care of Noya. She's my blood." He raises his eyebrows at Antoine. "I think there are other things you need to worry about."

Antoine glares at him but, notably, doesn't argue.

I look at Jeremiah. "Go." As he and Avery turn away, I take her arm. "Avery," I say awkwardly. "I'm sorry if I hurt you earlier. I was upset, and I wasn't thinking—"

"Yes, you were." She smiles at me sadly. "But I don't blame you. All of this is my fault. Connor will never forgive me, not after what has happened with Cass. I'll never forgive myself." She drops her head, the sheet of long hair hiding her face. "What are we going to tell Cass's mom, Harper?"

I shake my head. "I don't know. I guess we'll just have to work it out as we go. And Avery—it isn't your fault."

"Harper's right." Antoine says over my shoulder, looking at Avery. "Cass is a descendant of Samuel, the magician who bound Keziah. Keziah needed Cass's blood to break the binding holding her to our land. She already had yours. She's been planning this a long time, Avery. You were her tool, nothing more."

"How did Keziah know where the talismans were?" I ask Avery. It's been puzzling me ever since she told us her story.

"I saw them," says Avery, in a small voice. "Once, years ago, when Cass's mom was cleaning out the jewelry cabinet. She told me they were old family heirlooms from the slave days, and that people in her family thought they were magic. There was some family legend that if they were lost, the family would be cursed. Keziah must have pulled the information out of my head."

"The talismans were taken by Samuel, the magician who created the binding." Antoine's voice is gentle as he speaks to Avery. "He said he would hide them, keep them safe. He made a box for them, but he never told me where he put it, as a precaution against my ever being under Keziah's control again. I guess it's been handed down through the generations, but the significance of the talismans was lost over time."

Avery shakes her head. "I'm so sorry," she says, her voice breaking. "I'm so sorry for everything."

I move toward her but Jeremiah is already there, his arm protectively around Avery's shaking shoulders. He shoots me a warning glance. "I'll take her. We'll find Connor, Harper, don't worry." He leads Avery away, her head buried in his shoulder.

"Go." Tate speaks directly to Antoine. "I've got this, brother." He glances quickly at me and lowers his voice as he looks back at Antoine. "You need to drink."

Antoine makes an impatient noise. "And you need to leave here. You should never have come. It isn't safe."

Tate raises his eyebrows. "I think it's a little late for that," he says dryly. "And we both know you've never been good with new vampires." Antoine's fists clench so tightly that for a moment I'm worried he is about to plant one of them in Tate's face. But then the side of his mouth twitches upwards, and he tilts his chin.

"True," he says simply. Then his eyes fall on me, and the humor leaves his face. "You shouldn't have come here." His voice is rough. "Keziah could have taken you."

"And this is a conversation you should have somewhere else."

Tate turns to Noya's body. He pauses briefly and glances back at us. "But one question before you go, brother." A half smile plays on his mouth. "When Keziah called you, how did you resist?"

Antoine folds his arms. "I focused on something else," he says stiffly.

Tate's eyes slide to me then back to Antoine. He raises his eyebrows. "Hmm."

I think Antoine will reply, but he doesn't, and I can't read his expression. A moment later, he turns abruptly away, and we set off, leaving Tate with that same half smile still on his face.

Antoine and I walk down the mound, toward my car. Jeremiah and Avery are already gone. I look sideways at Antoine's set face. Though he's clearly recovered from the wolf bite, I know he must still be weak. "Tate's right," I say, as we come into the parking garage. "You need to drink, Antoine." I lean against my Mustang and hold up my hand. He looks at the dried line on my palm and his lips tighten.

"I never should have drunk from you," he says curtly. "And I never will again."

I feel something twist painfully inside me. "I know you regret everything that happened between us." I look away, unable to face the hard light in his eyes. "But the binding is broken. There's no reason for us to be married anymore." The lump in my throat is so thick I struggle to speak through it. "And no matter what Noya made you promise, I want you to know that I will never force you to stay here. I know that's why you resisted Keziah, because you feel responsible. But it isn't your job to protect us. To protect me." I take a deep breath. "I can't bear for that to be the reason you stay here." Despite my best efforts, my voice breaks on the last words. I force myself to raise my eyes to his, and what I see there takes my breath away.

His eyes are no longer the black of his illness, nor the hard, unforgiving slate that hurts so much. They are the storm-tossed purple of the man I married, and when, a moment later, the sun lights the gold in their depths, he is the blazing man I love, no matter how hard I've tried not to.

"You think I regret what has happened between us?" He's so close I can feel the heat of his body. "That I only married you for the binding, or that I came back because of a promise I made to someone else?"

"I don't know what to think," I whisper.

"Resisting Keziah's summons is the hardest thing I've ever done in my life." His hand comes up, cupping my face. "It was like having a hand on my heart, wringing the life from it. Every fiber in my body wanted to run to her, to be at her side. And do you know how I resisted it, Harper?" His thumb strokes my jaw. "I thought of you." His other hand comes up, and he holds my face so I can't look away. "I can't compel you, Harper," he says roughly, "so you need to listen to what I'm about to say and remember it." His eyes search my face. "One day, you will want a family. Children. A life free of demons in the cellar and wolves across the river. And I want that for you. I want you to live that human life, safe from all the horrors you found when your brother bought that damned, cursed mansion. No—" he says, when I start to protest. "You need to hear this." His hands tighten on my face. "I didn't leave here because I regret what happened between us. I left because being near you is impossible for me. I didn't marry you because of the damned binding, Harper. I married you because . . . as crazy and selfish and utterly irrational as it is, I love you. And I didn't come back because Noya made me promise to. I came back because every moment I was away from you I felt like a piece of me was missing, and it hurt so much I could barely breathe. It hurt more than any hold Keziah could ever have over me." He half smiles. "Missing you, believe me, is much harder than resisting Keziah ever could be."

I'm stunned into silence, oblivious to everything but the words he is saying and the way he is looking at me.

"But I will miss you again." His smile fades. "When this is over and you are out of danger, I will leave here—and this time, I won't come back." His hands stroke my face. "Not because I don't love you, Harper," he says quietly. "But because I love you so damn much I can't bear to watch you live that life with someone else. I'm not Tate. I have neither his strength, nor his honor. I can't watch you live that life with someone else, but I also won't be the selfish fool who takes it away from you."

"You didn't turn Tate into a vampire to punish him, did you?" A suspicion I've had for some time now is rising to the surface.

"No." Antoine meets my eyes, and for the first time since I've known him, I see behind the slate mask, down into the purple and gold storm of his soul. "What I did was far worse. I turned Tate because I couldn't stand the thought of living an eternity without him. And in doing so, I ruined his chance to have a normal life, and my only sister's happiness. I condemned my family to ruin and Tate to an eternity of pain. And I've run from him in shame every day since."

I reach up to touch his face. "But you haven't run this time," I whisper. "Not yet. You're not leaving yet."

Slowly, his head moves from side to side beneath my hand. "No," he says. "Not yet."

"Then we have this. We have now."

"Yes." He touches the emerald on my hand. "And whether I am with you or not," he says roughly, "no matter what happens, Harper—this is yours."

"Always," I breathe.

He nods. "Always."

And then he is kissing me, and I don't care what he says about leaving, because for now he is here, his arms holding me so hard against him I don't know where he leaves off and I begin, and everything I remembered about how it feels to be kissed by him is a lie, because this is better. It's cedar and sunlight and the scent of moonflowers on the grass, deeper and darker than the magnolia day on which we were married, because this is different.

This is love.

CHAPTER 22

STORM

*D*ear Tessa,

It's afternoon and I'm writing this on the dock by the river. Insects hang over the water, gleaming in the golden light. The air is still and thick, like the lull before a storm comes.

Antoine and Tate are gone hunting. I hope they're talking, that Antoine is telling Tate what he told me this morning. But Antoine and Tate have been alive a long time. They do things their own way, at their own pace. Maybe they're talking. Maybe they're just hunting, like they used to. I like to imagine them like that, running together somewhere upriver, laughing like the boys they once were.

Like brothers.

Antoine told me he'd be home before sunset. I figure I have some time left before then, and I needed to write to you, to feel you close.

Connor is gone, Tessa. I don't know where he is, or if he'll come home. Tate says he tracked him over the river, following the wolves, and found Connor's truck parked outside Remy's cabin by the water. Of Keziah, Cass, and Caleb, there's been no sign. They were gone from here before the sun was fully up.

Antoine says it will be days, if not weeks, before they come close again. It takes that long, he says, for a newborn vampire to learn any semblance of control.

I can't begin to imagine how Connor is feeling. I still don't know how I feel. I'm exhausted and exhilarated, heartbroken and in love, all at once. It's too much to feel and too soon to understand any of it.

All I know right now is that even though it's winter, the magnolia by the dock where I'm sitting has flowers still that smell sweet and comforting. They lean toward me as I write this, as if they want to touch my face, like you once did, in those last days.

You are here with me, Tessa, just as you always have been.

And I'm going to need you.

The still air isn't lying. A storm is coming. A bad one, Tessa. One that could destroy us all yet.

But at least Antoine and I will face it together.

I don't know very much anymore. But that, at least for now, is my truth. It is the only thing aside from you I have to hold on to.

It is my Always.

Your twin,

Harper

A SAMPLE OF POISON BERRY, THE NEXT BOOK IN THE Nightgarden Saga, continues on the following pages. You can also buy Poison Berry in the Amazon store to keep reading.

If you enjoyed Moon Vine, please consider leaving a review on Goodreads and/or Amazon. Reviews help sell books, and I can't tell you how much I appreciate them!

POISON BERRY SAMPLE

PROLOGUE

*D*ear Tessa,

    I'm writing this in the garden I made by the river, as the night jasmine opens beneath the stars. You gave me the seeds just before you went to hospital for the last time. You told me to plant them when I found a place to call home. Two weeks ago, the night after Cass became vampire, I mixed the last of your ashes with the seeds and put them in my night garden, here at the mansion.

You always said I could make anything grow. After you died, though, I stopped gardening. Something in me didn't feel able to put my hands in soil, cultivate anything. I think I was terrified of growing something, only to watch it die. I couldn't bear any more death.

That has changed since we came here.

Now, I'm learning to accept death, to live with it. To understand that even in death, there is life; that in the most toxic of plants, there is a gift. Night jasmine is poisonous, and yet it is a secret, exotic delight.

I refuse to fear death anymore.

My night garden is how I survive the long hours when

Antoine is gone, Connor is god alone knows where, and my beautiful friend Cass is out there somewhere, lost in the darkness. My night garden is where I go to restore my own soul, to feel the warm river earth beneath my fingers and reassure myself that somehow, we will survive all of this.

I know Antoine loves me. He can't hide that anymore, and it is a miracle no less than the flowers that open beneath the moon that he feels even part of what I do for him. But even love will not keep him at my side when this is over, and Cass is rescued. In the moments we are together I forget Cass, I forget everything. I feel guilty that I can be so happy when so much is crumbling around us.

None of us have seen Cass since the day she was made, though we've heard plenty. She has joined Keziah and Caleb, the vampires who spent the past three hundred years bound in the cellar of the Marigny mansion. Now the bind that held them captive is broken. The trio crossed the river into Louisiana the day Cass was made. Since then, they've cut a bloodthirsty swathe through the riverside towns, leaving a trail of unsolved murders and drained bodies in their wake. The nightly news has begun to talk about 'deadly gang wars' and 'strange cult rituals'.

The only thing holding them in check is the newborn wolf pack from the bayou, led by Remy. The bite from a wolf must be dangerous even to Keziah, for she runs from their scent. The pack roam the perimeter of the bayou towns, trying to protect as much ground as possible. Without their presence, I suspect the news would have a lot more bodies to talk about.

Despite what the wolves report, I can't equate the sweet, quiet Cass who has been my friend since I came to Deepwater with the fierce monster everyone talks of. I'm not blind to the manner of creature she is now. I saw the savagery in her face the morning Antoine wrought the sun magic in her body. I just think there's more to what she is than the monster they talk of, is all.

Antoine blames himself for what she has become. He and Tate have tried to track Keziah, but Antoine says she knows all too well how to hide, even from him, who she made. Keziah doesn't summon him anymore. Antoine says that is because now she has Cass, a tool she might wield at her own pleasure.

Connor is devastated by Cass's transformation. He blames himself as much as Antoine does, I think. But he doesn't speak of it, and whatever self-recrimination he suffers doesn't go any way to making him excuse Antoine's part. He can barely look at Antoine or me. Connor spends his nights driving the backroads of Louisiana, hoping, I guess, for a glimpse of the girl he loves, a chance to bring her home.

None of us have the heart to say the obvious - that even if by some miracle he was able to convince Cass to leave Keziah's side, she can never truly return. She will never be the schoolgirl she once was, planning college and a career. This transformation isn't some phase that will pass. Cass is a vampire. It isn't something that can be undone.

Keziah has compelled Selena, Cass's mom, to believe that Cass has gone to a music camp over in Biloxi for the winter term. Keziah has done a good job. Selena is excited and happy for Cass, and not at all bothered by her daughter's lack of communication.

Avery, too, blames herself for being the means by which Keziah broke out of the cellar. She's been trying to understand more about the power of her Natchez blood, and how she might use it, rather than have it used against her. Connor still won't speak to her. He won't speak to me, either. I don't know that he will ever forgive me for all the secrets I kept - especially the secret of my marriage to Antoine.

The nights are the hardest. Antoine and Tate roam far and wide in search of Cass. Connor does the same. And I wait at home, with only the distant howls of the wolves as comfort.

That's why I created a night garden. Planted in a half circle around a small pond, I filled it with seeds that grow only at night. Many of them are toxic, but that doesn't stop them being unutterably beautiful. I planted your seeds here. The books say jasmine blooms only in summer, but barely a week passed before the first flower burst open under the stars. Now their heady scent wends amid the moonvine and magnolias like a sensual dream. They thrive, and blossom, defying death, just as we do.

All I can do is hold onto the moments we have and try not to imagine the desert my life will be when Antoine is no longer here. Every time he leaves I can't help but feel he is preparing for a more final goodbye. I know that's why he doesn't spend his nights here, why he pulls away from me when I would pull him down onto my bed. He still holds onto the dream that I can have a normal life, one without a vampire husband, and wolves over the river.

For now, he has not annulled our marriage. For now, I am Harper Marigny, with the Marigny emerald on my wedding finger and a husband I love more than I ever dreamed possible.

You and I know happiness is fleeting, Tessa. I have to grasp it whilst Antoine is here, even if I do so whilst Connor is suffering, and Cass is become something we don't recognise.

The night jasmine is bursting into life under the new moon, and the red magnolias lie in a crushed carpet under my bare feet.

I am alive. I am loved. This is what I know.

I feel you here, with me, Tessa.

Your twin

Harper

POISON BERRY CHAPTER 1

MARRIAGE

$\mathcal{I}$ wake to an engine in the driveway, and voices murmuring in the kitchen. I lie in bed for a moment and savor the comforting sound of Antoine and Tate talking in the kitchen as they make coffee. I know they won't come upstairs. Tate respects my privacy, and Antoine, I suspect, doesn't trust himself anywhere near my bedroom. That thought should make me smile, but it doesn't.

Despite the fact that Antoine has barely left my side in the two weeks since Cass was made, I'm uncomfortably aware that he never allows himself to lose control with me. With the binding broken, there's no reason for Antoine and I to remain married. Keziah and Caleb are no longer held captive by the title deed to the mansion, and so there's no need for my name to be Marigny. Our marriage could be annulled today, the work of an instant.

I try to push the unsettling thoughts from my mind, smiling at the comforting chatter below. The smile fades after my shower when I'm pulling on denim shorts and a cotton top, listening out for Connor's voice. As usual, it isn't there. I put my head sound his door just to check. If the dirty clothes left on his bedroom floor are any indication, he returned yesterday when I was at school to wash and change, then left again. His absence makes me feel like part of myself is missing. His work on both the mansion and his construction business has come to an abrupt halt since Cass was turned. I've barely seen him. Connor is the only family I have left. The thought of life without him in it is too cold and lonely to even imagine.

I swallow my disappointment and walk downstairs to find Antoine and Tate leaning against the peeling ionic columns on the porch, sipping coffee in companionable silence. Since the night of Cass's transformation an odd truce seems to have developed between them, albeit an unspoken one. The thought of either of them opting for a serious heart to heart discussion of their emotions is enough to make me actually smile. Whether it's a product of the era into which they were born, or just their natures, two men less inclined to soul baring I can't imagine.

"I'm glad we amuse you." Antoine tugs gently at one of the flyaway curls bursting from the copper pile on my head. "What exactly is holding all that up?"

"A strategically placed pencil." I reach for the coffee, passing by a little closer than I need to. His eyes narrow. I feel the giddy rush of power I'm still not accustomed to, a thrill at the knowledge that he wants me. Perhaps not as much as I do him, but enough, at least, that he finds my nearness disturbing.

Tate is smirking into his coffee. I turn away to hide the colour in my face.

"You didn't find Cass, did you." I sip my coffee, my words a statement rather than a question.

"No." Antoine's reply is equally terse.

Every morning I ask the same thing. Every morning Antoine has the same answer.

"What about Connor?" I try to keep my voice even. This time there is a short pause, then Tate answers.

"No, Harper. We didn't see Connor."

We didn't see Connor. Not 'didn't find' Connor, I note. *Didn't see.* It's a slight difference, but one I notice, just as I notice that every morning it is Tate who answers that particular question, not Antoine.

They know where my brother is. They just won't tell me. And Antoine can't bring himself to actually lie to me, so Tate does it for him.

Every day we all pretend these exchanges are normal, because right now all we have is the illusion of normalcy to cling to, and sometimes, I guess, a lie or two is a small price to pay to maintain the fiction.

"Well—I'd better go." Tate pushes off the column and heads out to his truck, pretending not to notice the high colour on my face, or my lack of invitation to stay for breakfast. He swapped out his flashy rental convertible for an old pick up a couple of days after Cass left. I take that to mean he plans to stay in Deep-water awhile. "Things to do," he says as he opens the truck door, but I see the flash of a crooked smile as he climbs inside and pulls away.

I can almost feel Antoine's storm-tossed eyes on my back. "Do you want some pancakes before I go?" I try to keep my voice steady. "I can mix some up—" I don't get any further before Antoine's arm snakes around my waist, pulling me hard against him. "I don't want pancakes," he says, with a half-smile. He reaches up and plucks the pencil from my hair, sending the mass of curls tumbling chaotically down my back.

"That's better." His hand twines in my hair and his mouth is on mine, and it's lucky I already put my coffee cup down because I cannot tell what way is up anymore. One large hand is splayed at the base of my spine, and there is only denim and thin cotton between him and I. His mouth moves away and I press against him, my lips on his neck, and then he puts his head back and takes a deep breath, his hands slipping down to hold me loosely by the hips, putting an unwelcome distance between us. My body arches toward him as if it has a will of its own. "Come upstairs."

He ducks his head in a reluctant negative. "I can't, Harper." He strokes the hair down my back. "We can't."

"Yes, we can." I hide my face against his neck. "We're married."

I've never dared say it aloud before. I feel him tense against me, then his jaw hardens as he turns away.

"We need to go. You'll be late to class." His tone is slightly rough. I can feel the tension in his body, the stillness of the hands that only a moment ago roamed freely all over me. "Get your things." He's out of reach, now. "I'll drive. And take something to eat on the way."

When I come back out from the kitchen, Antoine has his hands on his hips, feet apart, staring moodily down the slope toward the night garden.

"The plants are starting to bloom already," I say.

"It's just gone midwinter. Those magnolia trees shouldn't have flowers." He glares at them accusingly.

"Things just seem to grow here." I put my bag over my shoulder. I don't mention Tessa's ashes in the soil, or my fanciful belief that my twin somehow talks to me through the trees and plants here. We have enough crazy around us without my imagination taking hold.

"I haven't felt like painting, lately." I glance guiltily at the library where my half-finished mural lies abandoned on one wall. I can't so much as bring myself to look at it. All I can think of when I do is Cass's lifeless body lying on the floor beneath it. "Gardening is what I'm doing instead."

Our eyes meet for a moment, and Antoine's soften. He puts his arm around me, and I lean against his comforting strength as we go toward his truck.

Halfway into Deepwater, the sun is gleaming off the slow,

brown river when I speak again. "The Legacy Committee's Midwinter ball is on in a few weeks."

"A bit late, isn't it? Midwinter was a fortnight ago."

I shrug. "I guess they can't hold a ball during the holidays." I take a breath. "Would you go with me?"

He shoots me a quizzical glance. "A ball, Harper?"

"Connor is their grant winner for this year. He's supposed to be the guest of honor. I know he was going to take Cass. Now . . . well, I guess we both know that isn't possible. I can make up some excuse for Connor. But one of us should go. It's expected." I look out the window to hide the color in my face. "I'd like it if you came with me."

When I look back, Antoine's smile has gone and he's shaking his head. "That isn't a good idea, Harper."

My heart sinks. "Why not?" Perhaps it's the recollection of his earlier lack of control, but I feel a little reckless, tired of all that lies unspoken between us. "What are you so afraid of, Antoine?"

He doesn't answer until we pull into the lot at school. He gets out of the truck and slams his door with unnecessary force, then comes around and wrenches mine open. I stand up, fold my arms and meet his hard stare with my own. "Well?"

"Three hours ago, Harper, what do you think I was doing?" He puts one hand on the truck behind me. I'm leaning against it, and he is so close I can inhale the cedar scent of him. It makes my senses whirl.

"I don't know." I try to shrug.

"Then let me tell you." He leans forward, and despite the fact that we are in a public lot, my body is already reacting to his nearness, swaying toward him, and I catch my breath as he puts his mouth so close to my ear I can feel the touch of his lips on my skin. "Three hours ago," he murmurs, "I was compelling a drunken man outside a roadhouse to let me drink his blood, and then to forget he'd ever seen me. When I'd finished with him, I was still thirsty, so I found a woman who was sad and tired and had nowhere to go, and then I drank from her. A few hours from now she will wake to find herself in a cheap motel with fifty dollars she didn't know she had, a little dizziness, and a strange resolution that she never wants to drink alcohol again. That's what I was doing three hours ago, Harper, while you were sleeping in your bed and dreaming of Midwinter balls." He pulls back and his eyes are dark steel on mine. "Now do you see why going to a ball with me is a bad idea?"

I feel the intensity of his words, the dark scenes they evoke. My hands go up to hold his face. "You say those things as if they should scare me." I search his eyes. "But you drank from me, remember? I'm not afraid of you, Antoine. I'm not frightened by what you do to survive."

"You should be." He steps back, taking my hands from his face and holding them in his own. "What we do to exist isn't a game, Harper. Even if I have sworn never to drink from you again, you need to know that. To really understand what it means."

I frown, about to say it was my choice to give him my blood, one I would make again, when a sharp voice interrupts us.

"Miss Ellory. The school parking lot is not a nightclub." It's Mr Larkin, the tightly buttoned history teacher, and he's glaring at Antoine and I as if we were naked and horizontal. Avery and Jeremiah are standing behind him, openly laughing at us.

"I'm sorry, Mr Larkin." Aware that half the lot is watching, I step away from Antoine, who is looking at Mr Larkin with a half-smile and folded arms, as if daring the teacher to say something else.

"I'll pick you up this afternoon, Harper." He's loud enough to be heard by the entire lot.

"Hmph." Mr Larkin glares at him. "I hardly think Harper's brother would approve of someone your age collecting her from class, Mr—"

"Marigny," Jeremiah interjects, grinning. "Antoine Marigny is my guardian, Mr Larkin."

"Your guardian?" Mr Larkin looks Antoine up and down disapprovingly, taking in the faded denims, loose linen shirt, and insolent grin. "You're a little young to be a guardian, don't you think, Mr Marigny?"

Antoine cocks his head at the teacher. "Well now that's funny. Weren't you just saying I was a little too old to be collecting Harper from class?" Raising his eyebrows quizzically, Antoine moves around to the driver's side door. Then he pauses and turns back. A moment later his mouth is on mine, hard and deep enough to set my skin aflame and make every kid in the lot hoot and whistle. When he finally pulls back, he grins down at me. "Behave." He nods at Mr Larkin. "And you be certain to have yourself a nice day, now." Swinging himself into the truck he murmurs, "I've never been great at authority." He pulls out of the lot with a jaunty wave, leaving a glowering Mr Larkin in his wake as he drives away.

I walk inside between Avery and Jeremiah, a warm feeling in my chest. Mr Larkin follows us, still glaring over his shoulder at the dust haze left by my husband's truck.

POISON BERRY CHAPTER 2

MONSTERS

"*W*ay to be subtle," says Avery on the way to history, but she's smiling. It's good to see her smile. Lately all I've seen are furrowed brows and worry. "So you and Antoine are pretty serious, huh?"

I make a non-committal sound and look studiously ahead. She casts an assessing eye over the knotted mass of hair falling down my back, and my flushed face. "Uh huh. So have you slept with him yet?"

"Avery!" I'm going for shocked, but it's Avery, so she just raises her eyebrows and waits for an answer.

"No." I stare at the floor, my face flaming for the second time that morning.

"Why not?" She gives me a side eye. "You're married, aren't you?"

"Avery!" This time I'm not faking the shock. I drop a book with a clatter and look around to see if anyone heard her. "It's more complicated than that," I hiss.

"Is it?"

I can feel her eyes on my back as I pick the book up, and I'm glad when Mr Larkin passes by, glaring at us both. I scurry inside and take my seat, which is thankfully out of Avery's line of sight. I don't know how to answer her questions. I don't understand the answers to them myself.

Jeremiah leans over the aisle. "Don't mind Avery. She's still getting used to—" his eyes drop to the emerald on my finger "— you know."

"Oh, I know," I mutter. Avery's not the only one getting used to it. I just don't want the entire senior class to be getting used to it, as well.

The class is still clattering books and pens when the door opens again and an odd silence falls across the room.

"What the *actual* French Toast," hisses Jeremiah beside me.

I look up and freeze.

Standing in the door, looking like three improbably perfect models dropped from a Parisienne catwalk, are Keziah, Cass, and Caleb.

Only the gleaming, glamorous figure standing between the other two isn't the Cass I knew. And by the shocked expressions on the faces of the rest of the class, it isn't the Cass they remember.

I don't think she's actually taller than she was. Perhaps it's her slick braids that make it seem that way, coiled into an intricate crown that towers high on her head. Or maybe it's the black silk dress she wears, dropping in sheer perfection to mid gleaming thigh. *No—it's the heels,* I realise. All sleek six inches of them. Nobody wears heels like that to school. Before today, I don't think I've ever seen Cass wear heels at all. Or, a silk dress, for that matter. The diamond and gold thread earrings falling down her neck look real, as does the matching ring on her hand. But it's really her eyes that stand out.

The last time I saw them they were blood red, fierce and strange, the eyes of a predator. I'm not sure what she's done to tame them, but now they are the gleaming, savage gold of a great cat. They look disdainfully across the classroom, passing over both Avery and I as if we weren't there at all. Perhaps it's my growing familiarity with supernatural creatures that makes me notice the shimmering, shifting light in their depths, a strange iridescence, like an oil slick on water. Antoine's is purple and gold, like sun behind clouds, where Cass's gleam crimson and gold, like mixed metals.

"Mr Larkin?" Keziah's voice sends a shiver down my spine. It's familiar from the long ago dreams when she sought access to my mind, with a faint accent that I can't quite place, and a certain old fashioned cadence that, given her age, is unsurprising. "The registrar sent us here. I'm Keziah Joseph, and this is my brother, Caleb. We're Cass's cousins. She's been visiting with us in Biloxi for a time."

AFTERWORD

Buy Poison Berry in the Amazon store to keep reading.

If you enjoyed Moon Vine, please consider leaving a review on Goodreads and/or Amazon. Reviews help sell books, and I can't tell you how much I appreciate them!You can read Antoine's story, a prequel to the Nightgarden Saga, here. It is free and exclusive to readers!

Follow me on tiktok @paulaconstant.

Listen to the playlist that accompanies the Nightgarden Saga.

You can also join the Nightgarden Readers Facebook group, and chat with others (and me) about the series.

If you'd like to be the first to read new Lucy Holden work, why don't you join my advance reader team? You can sign up on my website at www.paulaconstant.com/the-nightgarden-saga.com.

ABOUT THE AUTHOR

Lucy Holden is the pen name under which author Paula Constant writes paranormal romance. She is also the author of historical fiction series The Visigoths of Spain, and of travel memoirs Slow Journey South, and Sahara.

Paula lives in Broome, a tropical pearling town in North West Australia, and loves drinking wine beneath a full moon on the beach and dreaming up new book ideas.

www.paulaconstant.com

Printed in Australia
AUHW021319271021
354375AU00078B/544